Also From Kristen

Bayou Magic:
Shadows
Spells
Serendipity

The Curse of the Blue Moon:
Hallows End
Cauldrons Call
Salems Song

The Big Sky Series:
Charming Hannah
Kissing Jenna
Waiting for Willa
Enchanting Sebastian
Enticing Liam
Taunting Callum
Honor
Courage

Kristen Proby's Crossover Collection:
Soaring With Fallon: A Big Sky Novel by Kristen Proby
Wicked Force: A Wicked Horse Vegas/Big Sky Novella by Sawyer Bennett
All Stars Fall: A Seaside Pictures/Big Sky Novella by Rachel Van Dyken
Hold On: A Play On/Big Sky Novella by Samantha Young
Worth Fighting For: A Warrior Fight Club/Big Sky Novella by Laura Kaye
Crazy Imperfect Love: A Dirty Dicks/Big Sky Novella by K.L. Grayson
Nothing Without You: A Forever Yours/Big Sky Novella by Monica Murphy

The Fusion Series:
Listen To Me
Close To You
Blush For Me

The Beauty of Us
Savor You

The Boudreaux Series:
Easy Love
Easy Charm
Easy Melody
Easy Kisses
Easy Magic
Easy Fortune
Easy Nights

The With Me In Seattle Series:
Come Away With Me
Under the Mistletoe With Me
Fight With Me
Play With Me
Rock With Me
Safe With Me
Tied With Me
Burn With Me
Breathe With Me
Forever With Me
Stay With Me
Indulge With Me
Love With Me
Dance With Me
Dream With Me
You Belong With Me
Imagine With Me
Escape With Me
Flirt With Me
Take a Chance With Me

Huckleberry Bay:
Lighthouse Way
Fernhill Lane
Chapel Bend

Cherry Lane

Single in Seattle:
The Secret
The Surprise
The Scandal
The Score
The Setup

The Love Under the Big Sky Series:
Loving Cara
Seducing Lauren
Falling For Jillian
Saving Grace

From 1001 Dark Nights:
Easy With You
Easy For Keeps
No Reservations
Tempting Brooke
Wonder With Me

The Romancing Manhattan Series:
All the Way
All It Takes
After All

Cherry Lane
A Huckleberry Bay Novella
By Kristen Proby

1001 DARK NIGHTS
PRESS

Cherry Lane
A Huckleberry Bay Novella
By Kristen Proby

1001 Dark Nights
Copyright 2023 Kristen Proby
ISBN: 979-8-88542-025-9

Foreword: Copyright 2014 M. J. Rose

Published by 1001 Dark Nights Press, an imprint of Evil Eye Concepts, Incorporated

Sign up for the 1001 Dark Nights Newsletter
and be entered to win a Tiffany Key necklace.

There's a contest every month!

Go to www.1001DarkNights.com to subscribe.

**As a bonus, all subscribers can download
FIVE FREE exclusive books!**

One Thousand and One Dark Nights

Once upon a time, in the future…

*I was a student fascinated with stories and learning.
I studied philosophy, poetry, history, the occult, and
the art and science of love and magic. I had a vast
library at my father's home and collected thousands
of volumes of fantastic tales.*

*I learned all about ancient races and bygone
times. About myths and legends and dreams of all
people through the millennium. And the more I read
the stronger my imagination grew until I discovered
that I was able to travel into the stories… to actually
become part of them.*

*I wish I could say that I listened to my teacher
and respected my gift, as I ought to have. If I had, I
would not be telling you this tale now.
But I was foolhardy and confused, showing off
with bravery.*

*One afternoon, curious about the myth of the
Arabian Nights, I traveled back to ancient Persia to
see for myself if it was true that every day Shahryar
(Persian: شهريار, "king") married a new virgin, and then
sent yesterday's wife to be beheaded. It was written
and I had read that by the time he met Scheherazade,
the vizier's daughter, he'd killed one thousand
women.*

Something went wrong with my efforts. I arrived in the midst of the story and somehow exchanged places with Scheherazade – a phenomena that had never occurred before and that still to this day, I cannot explain.

Now I am trapped in that ancient past. I have taken on Scheherazade's life and the only way I can protect myself and stay alive is to do what she did to protect herself and stay alive.

Every night the King calls for me and listens as I spin tales. And when the evening ends and dawn breaks, I stop at a point that leaves him breathless and yearning for more. And so the King spares my life for one more day, so that he might hear the rest of my dark tale.

As soon as I finish a story... I begin a new one... like the one that you, dear reader, have before you now.

Prologue

Cherry

"My new neighbor just pulled in." I'm on the phone with my best friend, Montana, as I peer through the slats of my blinds, waiting for the driver to hop out of the moving truck below. "I'm hoping for an older lady or someone single. And quiet."

"*You're* an old lady," Montana replies with a chuckle. "And you're not even thirty yet. You need to learn to live a little."

"I work super early in the morning," I remind her. "And the last people watched old western movies late into the night. It was either that, or there were shoot-outs next door. Either way, it wasn't fun."

"I'm hoping it's someone *hot*," Montana replies. "A hot man who's going to come in there and sweep you off your feet and remind you what it's like to be young and spontaneous."

"Was I *ever* young and spontaneous?"

"It's not too late to start now. Hey, I've got some customers. I'd better go. Keep me posted."

"Will do. Save some of that huckleberry ice cream for me."

As I set my phone aside, the moving truck's door opens, and I hold my breath, waiting.

"What is taking so long?" I mutter. "Step out, damn it. Show yourself."

It's hot today, which is unusual for Huckleberry Bay. Being a seaside town, we get a lot of ocean breeze, but the air is still today, and the sun is blazing.

I'm almost sticky.

I could turn on the air-conditioning, but I'm cheap as hell.

Finally, I see a sneaker-clad foot sticking out of the truck, then blue jeans appear.

And then…I sigh as I see that Montana got her wish.

He's sexy as hell and just upped the temperature in here by ten degrees, making me rethink the air-conditioning situation. I can't help but notice he has no ring on his finger.

And he fills out a white T-shirt nicely with muscled arms and a chest that begs for a woman's hands.

He has sunglasses on, aviators at that, so I can't see his eyes. But his hair is brown, and it's messy, like he's been running his hands through it in agitation.

"Shit. He's hot. Am I going to have to listen to him have sex all the time? I mean, looking like that, he must have women falling at his feet. Or, he's attached."

Scowling, I blow out a breath and step back from the blinds, deciding to go down and introduce myself.

I might as well see what I'm getting into with the new neighbor.

Slipping my feet into my old, pink flip-flops, I walk down the stairs to the parking lot and catch Mr. Sexypants as he opens the back of the truck.

"Hey."

He glances at me in surprise and then slowly pulls his glasses down his nose and looks me up and down, a smile spreading over his face.

He's not hot.

He's *devastating*.

"Hi," he says in reply.

"Are you moving into 2F?"

"That's me." He leans back on the truck and folds his arms over his chest. "Am I lucky enough to have you as a neighbor?"

"Yeah. I'm 2D, across from you. I tried to buy your unit so I'd have the ocean view, but your offer came in higher than mine."

The smile doesn't waver.

"I can't say I'm sorry."

"At least you're honest. What's your name?"

"Zeke. What's yours?"

"Cherry."

That makes his eyebrows climb. "Your name is *Cherry*?"

"And yours is *Zeke*."

"Touché."

"I'd ask if I can help with anything, but I don't want to."

That makes him laugh. "Can't say I blame you. I don't want to, either. I have some friends coming to help in a little while. I thought I'd get the lay of the land before they got here. Feel like giving me a tour?"

"Have you never been here before?"

He shakes his head and walks toward me, which makes me take a step back. "I've been to Huck Bay, but no, I bought the place sight unseen. But I saw pictures online."

"First of all, it's *Huckleberry* Bay. No one calls it Huck. And second, you bought a whole house without ever stepping inside of it?"

"To be fair, it's a condo." He winks at me, and it immediately puts my back up, mostly because I'm still irritated that he bought this place out from under me. I don't want him to be flirty. "And I've been across the country for work and couldn't get out here to look. My realtor, Indigo, told me I should move on it because there was another offer on the place."

"Yeah." I glare at him. I can't help it. "*Mine.*"

"Oops. Come on, how about that tour?"

Begrudgingly, after kicking at some rocks, I follow behind him, climbing the stairs. Zeke has a great ass, nicely displayed in those jeans. It's a pity I already don't like him.

"Your unit is there," I say, pointing to my right before turning to my unit just across from his. "I'm there. Goodbye."

"Whoa. That's not very neighborly."

"You don't need me to show you anything."

"But I *want* you to," he says and gestures with that chiseled chin for me to follow him inside. "Come on. Let's have a look."

"How do I know you're not some kind of serial rapist, and this is how you lure women into your den to have your way with them?"

That makes him stop, and he seems to consider. "I guess you don't know that for sure. But for the record, I'm not."

With another sexy wink, he walks inside his condo, leaving the door open so I can enter.

"Damn it." I can't help but follow him in. I *love* this unit. When I bought my place several years ago, it was the only unit available, and I made myself a promise that when an ocean-view condo opened up, I'd snatch it up for myself.

But that didn't happen.

"This kitchen is real nice," Zeke says when he sees that I've followed him inside, a satisfied grin on his ridiculously handsome face. "Better than the pictures. And look at this. There's a view of the water from every room. How killer is that?"

"Yeah." I lean against the counter as Zeke walks through the rest of the two-bedroom condo, letting my resentment simmer in the back of my throat. "I know. Killer."

I shouldn't have come over here. It only makes me sad and wish with all my might that I'd taken that third job so I could afford to bid higher on this place. Maybe even a *fourth* job.

But I just couldn't make it work. There are only so many hours in a day, and as much as I hate to admit it, a girl has to sleep.

Plus, the price of these units is only going up. Condos are scarce in this town—especially oceanside ones. And, much to my dismay, Huckleberry Bay has become the tourist mecca of the west coast, so these units get snatched up by those who want to offer them as short-term rentals.

Thankfully, our homeowners' association put a stop to that last year.

"I definitely didn't go wrong with this purchase," Zeke says as he walks out of the main bedroom. "What do I need to know?"

"About what?"

"The complex. The neighborhood. Hell, Huckleberry Bay in general if you feel like sharing."

"It's awful. The whole town is the armpit of America. Crime is super high. There are a lot of fights and yelling. And animal sacrifices."

"Right." He's still smiling, and now I want to both hug and smack him. "You're trying to scare me off, but it won't work."

"Too bad for me, isn't it? Where did you move here from?"

"All over the place. Came because I'm opening a new business with my buddy, Wolfe."

"The garage?" I feel my eyebrows climb in surprise. I don't know Wolfe well, but I know he's going to turn the old garage in town into a *really* great new business. One that we all need desperately, so we don't have to drive more than an hour away for vehicle repairs.

If he's going into business with Wolfe, Zeke must be a smart man.

"You've already heard about it?"

"Of course. It's a small town. Well, good luck with the new business and everything. I'm sure it'll be great. You don't happen to like loud music, do you?"

"The louder, the better."

"Great. Just great."

Chapter One

One Year Later
Cherry

I can't *wait* to shower and get this gunk out of my hair. The annual Halloween party at Annabelle's big house up on the hill was a ton of fun. That woman knows how to throw an epic party, and this year was no different.

The theme was the roaring twenties, which meant I got to wear a pretty, sparkly dress, a bunch of makeup, and plaster my hair with hairspray in precise waves around my face. Don't even get me started on the glitter.

All the glitter in the land.

So, the first order of business after that fun party is a long, hot shower.

It'll be the perfect way to end a great night. I don't usually stay up until almost midnight, certainly not when I have to work so early the next day, but it was worth every minute I stayed up past my bedtime. In addition to a fantastic evening spent with most of my friends in my little town, I got a couple of good digs in with Zeke, too. And from the look on his too-handsome face, it irritated the hell out of him.

No regrets.

Since he'd moved in over a year ago, Zeke and I have settled into a nice routine of mutual dislike, verbal jabs, and looks that could kill at fifty paces.

I'm still bitter that he bought the condo out from under me. But more than that, I'm tired of watching so many people like him move into my sleepy little town and try to *change it.*

Just last week, he complained to me down by the mailboxes that there isn't a decent place to get Mexican food without driving fifty miles.

People think they would love to live here, but then move in and do nothing but complain because it doesn't have the conveniences of the big city.

It's annoying as hell.

Blowing out a breath, I open my music app and choose soothing songs to listen to during my shower. Next, I light a candle that I made myself and offer for sale online, and then turn on the water to let it heat up.

Humming under my breath, I make a trip to the linen closet to grab a towel and a hair wrap. Once I've stripped down and hung my dress in the closet, I return to the shower.

It's not steamy yet, but it'll get there, so I step in and shiver.

"That's *cold.*" Moving out of the direct line of the spray until it heats up, I decide to start with shaving my legs.

But the more I lather them up, the more I realize that the shower isn't getting any warmer, no matter how far I turn the nozzle to the red side.

"Shit," I mutter. "Is the hot water out?"

I step out of the shower and wrap my towel around myself. Without thinking, I stomp out the front door, shaving cream running down my legs, and mascara streaking my face, and head over to Zeke's apartment to knock on the door.

A few seconds later, he opens it. His eyebrows climb in surprise when he sees that it's me and takes in the state I'm in.

"Is your hot water out?"

"Huh?"

"I was trying to shower,"—I gesture to myself—"and I don't have any hot water. Is yours out, too?"

"Is this a trick question?"

"Shit, it's cold out here." I start to bounce in place, leaving a little shaving-cream-laced puddle on the floor, and scowl at him. "Check your water, please."

"It doesn't work like that." He shakes his head and smiles as he leans on the doorjamb and crosses his arms over his chest, clearly enjoying himself as his eyes journey down my wet body.

"If you laugh at me, I'll poke your eyes out."

"Have you always been such a violent woman? Look, each unit has its own hot water heater, Cherry. It's not like when the electricity goes out for the whole building."

"Damn it. The one night a year that it's not going to be a quick shower, this happens. I *hate* cold showers." Shivering, I start to turn and slosh back to my place.

"Use mine."

He offers so easily it makes me blink.

"You don't want me in your shower."

"I don't mind." He shrugs as if he has women in his shower all the time—which he probably does. "Seriously, go get your stuff. I'll start it for you."

I stay planted where I am and narrow my eyes at him until he huffs out a breath and physically turns me around.

"Go. Get your stuff. I'll leave the door open for you."

I should decline, suck it up, and just take the cold shower. But it will take me at least three shampoos to get all the gunk out of my hair, then I need to condition, and I don't want to do all of that in cold water.

So, without overthinking it, I hurry back to my bathroom, blow out my candle, gather my hair stuff, razor, soap, hair wrap, and then grab some clothes before rushing back over to Zeke's place. True to his word, the door is open, so I walk right in and head straight for the guest bathroom.

But the water isn't on there.

"Where are you?" I call out.

"My room," he calls back.

The main bathroom is already steamy from the shower when I walk in.

"I can use your guest bath."

"This one is better," he says with a shrug. "Bigger shower. Take your time."

He moves to pat me on the shoulder just as I turn, and rather than my shoulder, his hand lands right on my boob.

"Sorry," he says, jumping back. "I didn't mean—sorry."

He hurries out the door, closes it, and leaves me wondering what in the ever-loving hell just happened.

Zeke *never* fumbles or seems unsure of himself. If anything, he's a cocky, arrogant ass. But one accidental touch of *my* breast, and he fumbles away?

Talk about a shot to my ego.

I drop my towel and step into the blessedly hot water. Then, deciding to start fresh, I rinse off completely and begin with my hair.

It takes *four* shampoos until glitter no longer runs down the drain, and when I finally have the conditioner on, I turn my attention to my legs.

I forgot my shaving cream, so I use Zeke's. The smell of him fills the steamy room, making my stomach clench. How is it that he annoys the crap out of me, yet I want to climb him like a damn tree all at the same time?

Finally, feeling warm and clean, I turn off the water and wrap my hair to dry. I reach for my towel that I dropped on the floor, but then I realize that Zeke set out a fresh one for me and decide to use that one.

Once I'm dry and dressed, my hair still in its wrap, I emerge from the bathroom feeling a million times better and find Zeke in the kitchen, stirring something in a mug.

"I made this for you," he says, holding out the steaming cup. His eyes don't quite meet mine.

"What is it?"

"Hot chocolate."

"Thank you." I accept the offering and take a sip, then blink in surprise. "This didn't come out of a packet."

"No, ma'am. Melted it on the stove."

"You know how to make *real* hot chocolate?"

"Learned from my grandma," he confirms and sips from his own mug. "Did you have fun tonight?"

"I always have fun at Annabelle's Halloween party. It's the event of the year, you know."

"I've heard. This was my first one."

"Did you like it?"

"It was pretty amazing," he confirms. "But it seemed like most of the town was there. What do the kids do for trick-or-treating?"

"There are different events for them in town, usually earlier in the evening so their parents can go to Annabelle's party." I take a sip, delighting in the sweet warmth. "Work is going to *suck* for me tomorrow. I'm already dreading it."

I blow out a breath as Zeke tilts his head, watching me. "I've lived across from you all this time, and I don't know what you do for a living."

"We don't usually have civil conversations." I shrug one shoulder as if it doesn't matter. "I'm a preschool teacher, and I work the early shift. I have to be there by six-thirty so parents who go in early can drop their kids off before they head in."

"Damn, that's early."

"Why do you think I hate loud music at night?"

He nods slowly. "Makes sense. From now on, I promise to shut it down by nine."

I snort and set my now-empty mug in the sink. "Thanks for your help tonight. I'll take your towel home and wash it."

"Appreciate it," he says, watching as I gather my things in my arms. "Want me to come have a look at your water heater?"

"Oh, you don't have to." I wave him off, ready to go home. I'm not sure how to handle Zeke when we're not sparring with each other.

"I'm pretty handy with those kinds of things," he says as he slips his feet into a pair of sneakers. "But it's your heater. Your call."

Honestly, if it saves me from spending several hundred dollars, I'll take all the help I can get. I don't have a new hot water heater in my budget right now.

"If you don't mind, I would appreciate it if you'd have a look."

He grins and sets his mug in the sink beside mine, rubbing his hands together in anticipation. "I don't mind. This is what I'm made for. Let's do it."

I lead the way over to my place and key in the code to unlock the door. I don't have to tell Zeke where the heater is since it's in the same spot in his condo. I busy myself putting my things away, dropping the towels into the washing machine but not starting it. Then I join Zeke at the hot water heater in the hallway closet.

"Why do you have duct tape right here?" He frowns.

"Oh, there was an issue once, and I just used duct tape to fix it. It worked."

"Fire hazard," he mutters as he tinkers with something. "I hate to be the bearer of bad news, but I think this one is dead, Cherry."

"Like, the *whole* unit?"

"Yep." He closes it up and turns to me. "You can definitely call in a professional for a second opinion, and you'll need one anyway to replace it, but it looks like it's all burned up in there. I unplugged it so it doesn't set anything on fire."

"Shit," I mutter and pull the wrap off my head, shaking out the wet strands of my dark hair. "Well, thanks for having a look. I guess I'll be washing everything in cold water for a while. Including myself."

"Don't be stupid." He scowls down at me. "Just come over to my place until you can get on someone's schedule. You can wash your stuff over there and shower. It's really no big deal for me, and it's just across the hall."

"Listen, I know we don't get along—despite this little moment of truce. You don't have to do this."

"It's true, you drive me crazy. But that doesn't mean I can't be neighborly." He pushes his hand through his hair in agitation. *This* is the Zeke I know. "Maybe we can work out a trade."

I take a step back, appalled. "No."

"Jesus, not *that* kind of trade, although you're hot as fuck, and I wouldn't complain."

I'm pretty sure my jaw just hit the floor. Zeke thinks *I'm* hot?

"I was thinking that maybe you could put a hold on the nagging while I offer you my hot water."

"I don't *nag.*"

He laughs and rubs his fingertips into his forehead like he's completely frustrated.

"You nag more than my grandmother, and that woman could have won an Olympic gold medal if it were a sport."

"What do I nag you about?" I prop my hands on my hips and narrow my eyes at him.

"What *don't* you nag me about?" He shakes his head. "'*Turn the music down, Zeke. Stop laughing so loud, Zeke. Jesus, Zeke, when was the last time you checked your mail? It's overflowing in your box. Zeke, you parked like crap again.*' I'm telling you, I get real sick and tired of my name."

I can only blink at him. Do I really sound like that? Do I bitch at him constantly?

"Well." I sound stiff as a board, but I can't help it. I'm mortified. "I will stop doing that. Thanks for bringing it to my attention. And thank you for the offer, but I'll pass. I can go to my parents' house. I appreciate your help tonight. Have a nice evening."

He frowns. "Now, you just sound like you have a stick up your ass."

"What do you want from me?" It comes out in an exasperated shout. "Christ Jesus, Zeke, have you ever considered that I nag because you do those things *all the goddamn time*, and it's inconsiderate? No, I'm sure you haven't. You just think I'm a tight-ass bitch who likes the sound of my own voice, not a human being who has jobs and responsibilities of her own. But it's fine. I'll keep my mouth shut from here on out and suck it up. I'll invest in some noise-blocking earbuds and park in the visitor parking so I don't have to deal with your shitty parking jobs. I really do appreciate you being so nice to me tonight. It was a pleasant surprise, but I won't expect it to continue. See you around."

"God, you're so damn exasperating."

"Same goes, *Zeke*."

We just stand there for several seconds, breathing hard and glaring at each other, and then the next thing I know, Zeke closes the gap between us, cups my face in his hands, and kisses me.

Like, *kisses* me.

It's hot and demanding, as if he's been thinking about doing it since the minute we met, and he has months-and-months-worth of pent-up sexual aggression to get out.

And, surprisingly, I don't mind at all.

Because as much as he makes me want to scream, he makes me *feel*. He's the sexiest man I've ever seen in my life, and now that his hands are on me, his *mouth* on mine, I don't want him to ever stop.

I press against him, chest to stomach, and invite more.

And he gives more.

Takes more.

It's the hottest kiss of my damn life.

Zeke growls—like, literally *growls*—and reaches down to cup my ass. He picks me up like I weigh nothing at all, and I wrap my legs around his waist as he sets me on the kitchen counter.

"How is it possible," I mutter as his mouth does incredible things to my neck, "that we can dislike each other so much and want to tear off each other's clothes at the same time?"

"I don't know, but I'm not mad about it."

Oh, I'm definitely not mad about it. How can I be when his hands make me shiver, and his mouth may as well have been sent from God Himself?

But then, just as his hands dive under my shirt, I start to overthink it all. Which is totally on brand for me, even if it is stupidly inconvenient right now.

"Zeke."

I don't push him away, but he must sense the hesitation in my voice because his head comes up, and he pins me with those bright blue eyes.

"You want me to stop, Cherry?"

"No." But I don't sound convinced.

He cups my cheek and softly brushes his thumb back and forth.

"It's okay," he says as he rests his forehead against mine. "Now, *I* need a cold shower."

I can't help but laugh and be grateful that he isn't a complete jerk who issues a guilt trip when a girl says *enough*—even though I didn't actually *say* it.

"I have a cold shower you can use."

That makes him grin. "Do I need to apologize?"

"No." I can't resist dragging my fingertips down his cheek. "It might be mortifying if you do."

"Good, because I'm *not* sorry. I've been thinking about doing that for more than a fucking year."

"Really? Even though I'm a nag?"

I grin when his eyes smolder with more lust.

"You're the hottest nag in the county. We might dislike each other, but the chemistry…it's almost mean."

"You have to go home now," I inform him. "Because I *do* have to work early, and it's going to suck with sugar-riddled little kids first thing in the morning. And if you don't go, I'll ask you to stay, and that's not a good idea."

"I have a long day tomorrow, too. So, I'd better go home and put on that loud metal music I sleep to."

"Don't make me poke your eyes out."

"So violent," he says again, but he's grinning as he steps away from me. "The code to my door is 3792. Just come in when you need to."

"I won't—"

Before I can finish, he closes my door behind him, and I'm left sitting on the kitchen counter, completely turned on and irritated at the same time.

Sounds about right when it comes to Zeke.

Chapter Two

Zeke

"You're pissy as hell today."

I roll out from under a Honda to see my best friend, Wolfe, scowling down at me.

"I didn't say anything."

"Exactly. The only time you shut up is when you're pissed off about something. What's wrong with you?"

I push back under the car and ignore him, but he grabs my foot and pulls me out again.

"What the fuck? I have work to do here, man."

"You've been this way for three days, and it's driving me fucking nuts. What's up?"

I blow out a breath and stand, wiping my hands on the rag that always hangs from my back pocket.

"Neighbor," is all I say.

"You two really need to stop sparring with each other. It's kind of childish, Zeke."

If only that were the reason I was sleep-deprived and therefore...*pissy*.

But that's not it at all.

Cherry's been in my condo every day for the past three days for showers, to wash her dishes, do her laundry. She's always there, because even if she's gone by the time I get home, I can still *smell* her in my space.

She's invaded every waking thought, and every single one of those centers around getting her naked and fucking her blind.

Not to mention, she hasn't nagged me *once* since the other night, and my masochistic ass kind of misses it.

I've lost my damn mind.

"You're quiet again."

"I just haven't been sleeping well," I lie easily. "It's not a big deal."

Wolfe narrows his eyes at me. We both know he knows I'm full of shit.

We've worked together for more than a decade. I was his chief mechanic when he raced cars professionally, and when he was forced to retire, we went into business together in his hometown of Huckleberry Bay. He's like a brother to me.

"You're full of it."

I can only laugh and shake my head. "Yeah, well, I don't have another story to tell you. It's lunchtime. Hungry?"

"Of course, I'm hungry."

"I'll go get some food for us. Walk off the mood. What do you want?"

"Burgers from Gordy's. I want a double."

"I'll be back."

I take off my coveralls, hang them on the hook inside the back door, and then walk out into the fall air.

It's breezy today, which is usual for this coastal town, but it's not raining. The yellow and red leaves are starting to fall, and the long walk to Gordy's is pleasant.

"Hey, Zeke!"

I glance over and wave at Dotty, the bookstore's owner, as she sets her sign out on the sidewalk.

"Hey, Dot! Have a great day."

She grins and goes back to what she was doing. In the past year, I've grown to know pretty much all the shop and restaurant owners in town, along with most of the people who work in those businesses. And they know me.

I'm a military brat, so my family never stayed in one place for long when I was growing up. And then, when I joined the racing circuit, I continued to travel.

This is the first time in my life that I feel as if I'm setting down roots, and I have to admit, I like it.

Huckleberry Bay feels like home.

Sunny, the long-time waitress at Gordy's, greets me with a big smile when I walk into the place. "Hey there, handsome. Want a table or a seat at the counter?"

"Neither. I'm going to take it to go for Wolfe and me."

"You betcha. You want your usuals?"

"He wants a double," I reply with a nod. "Otherwise, yeah, the usual."

I live in a place where the waitress knows what my *usual* is. It always surprises me. Every time.

"You got it. Go park your fine ass over at the counter, and I'll bring it out to you when it's ready."

The older woman winks at me, and then, smacking her gum, heads off to put my order in.

Just as I take a seat to wait, I see Sarah, my good friend's wife, carrying food to a table of customers. When she sees me, she grins and heads my way.

"What are you up to?" she asks.

"Grabbing lunch to go. I thought Tanner told me you don't work here anymore."

Sarah smiles and pushes a strand of blond hair off her cheek. "I fill in when they're short-handed. Today was one of those days, so here I am. I don't mind it, actually. Gets me out of my studio."

Sarah's a talented artist, and her paintings have taken off in popularity, selling for a pretty penny in Tanner's gallery.

"I'm gonna have to go see what your husband has in stock at the gallery. I think it's time to hang some art on my walls since I've been here for over a year now."

"You don't have *anything* on your walls?" She looks almost pained at the idea.

"I hate to break it to you, but it's not really a priority for most guys."

"Let me come over, take a look at the space, and I'll paint something for you."

I blink at her, surprised. "Sarah, you don't have to paint me something custom. I'm happy to buy a piece you've already done."

"You're basically family, Zeke. Trust me, this will be better."

I don't know what I did in a past life to deserve this awesome group of friends, but I'm grateful for it.

"You're welcome to come over after work if you want."

"Oh, this is so exciting." She grins, almost bouncing on her toes. "Yes, I want. I need a new challenging project. I'll text you when I'm off here."

"Great. Thanks, Sarah."

"No, thank *you*. This is great."

The bell in the kitchen rings, and she pats me on the shoulder.

"That's my order. I'll see you later."

No sooner does she walk away than Sunny hurries over to me carrying a big bag of food.

"That looks like more than two burgers and fries."

She grins. "I had them add a few things. You boys need the calories."

Sunny is a mother hen. "Thanks, ma'am. Put it on our tab?"

"Already done. Have a good day."

"You, too."

On my way back to the garage, I notice that the air has cooled, and some clouds are rolling in from the ocean. Looks like we might get a storm.

* * * *

"Jesus Christ, I'm not going to eat for a month," Wolfe groans as we stow our tools away, getting ready to lock up for the day. "Why did she send so much food?"

"We didn't *have* to eat it all," I remind him, also feeling stuffed to the brim.

"Yeah, well, we did. And I'm supposed to take Luna out to dinner tonight."

"You'll be a cheap date." I grin at him as we take our coveralls off and hang them up. "Have fun with your wife. Sarah's coming over to look at my condo so she can paint me something for it."

He raises an eyebrow. "That's pretty awesome."

"I know. She offered when I saw her earlier, and I didn't want to pass it up, you know?"

"Hell no, don't pass that up. Tell her hi for me."

"Will do. See you tomorrow."

I wave and move to my car, fire up the engine, and head home. When I reach the complex, I'm sure to park perfectly in the lines so I don't irritate Cherry. It's been nice not having her constantly irritated with me over the past few days.

On my way up the stairs, I meet the woman herself, carrying a huge tote full of smaller boxes, obviously meant for the post office.

The bundle is so big she can't see me, so I walk back down the stairs to get out of her way and wait.

"Why do I always think that I have to carry everything at once?" she mutters to herself. "It's too damn heavy."

"I don't want to startle you," I begin, but she lets out a little squeal anyway and almost drops the tote. "Shit, that's what I was trying to avoid."

I hurry up and take the tote from her, frowning at just how heavy it really is.

"Good God, what do you have in here? Rocks?"

"Candles," she says, catching her breath. "They're orders that I'm filling."

"You have a candle business?" I ask as I follow her to her car, still carrying the tote. "I thought you were a preschool teacher."

"I am," she says as she opens the back of her SUV and gestures for me to set the container inside. "I do both."

"That's a lot of work."

She grins and pushes a button, but the hatch doesn't close. "Damn it this thing is acting up again."

With a sigh, she pulls it down manually and closes it.

"I'll take a look at it for you."

"It's okay, it's just a pain. I can close it myself."

"If you have the button, it should work," I insist. "I'll check it out tomorrow."

"You don't have—"

"Are you this stubborn with everyone, or just me?" I interrupt.

Her mouth opens, then closes again, and that line between her eyebrows deepens with her scowl.

"I'm already imposing on you enough. I don't need you to fix my car."

"Cars are my thing." I shrug and watch as she walks to the driver' side door, feeling disappointed that she's leaving.

I'd like to talk with her some more.

"If you don't mind, I'd like to bring over some laundry this evening."

"I don't mind. I told you, come over whenever." And I mean it. I've started to *enjoy* her. I want to know more about her, like this whole candle business that I just found out about. When we're not fighting, Cherry's beautiful and smart, not to mention funny as hell. And I love that she has the patience to work with preschoolers. I never would have thought I'd say this, but I *want* her around.

"Yeah, but don't you have to do your own laundry sometimes?"

"I'll catch up with it this weekend." I open her door for her. "Do you need help with that at the post office?"

"I've got it, thanks."

And with that, she shuts the door and takes off.

"See you," I mutter and sigh as I turn back to the stairs. "Do I smell bad? That woman can't get away from me fast enough. Not good for the ego."

When I'm inside my condo, I text Sarah to let her know that she can come by anytime, and she quickly replies that she's on her way since she just left work.

So, I hurry up and wash my hands, and by the time I'm finished changing my clothes, the doorbell rings.

"Hey, Sarah," I say as I open the door.

"You have excellent timing," she says with a smile. "I had literally just sat in the car after work."

"I'm glad it was convenient for you. Come on in."

I step back, and Sarah walks inside, then whistles. "I know I have my own water view, but it never gets old, does it?"

"No, it doesn't."

"Do you want a seascape?" she asks, pacing around my living room, taking everything in. "Like, on this wall here, above the sofa? I could do a nice big seascape, and then it'll feel like you're surrounded by the ocean. But if you want something different, I totally get it. I can do a meadow, a forest, you name it."

"Hmm." We stand together in the middle of the room, shoulder to shoulder, pondering it. "It really would look cool if there was an ocean scene up there to mirror what's going on outside."

"Right? I couldn't agree more." Sarah walks over to the windows, taking in my view. "So, I can make the painting look exactly like this,"—she points outside—"or I can switch it up."

"Let's switch it up."

"I was hoping you'd say that." She smiles up at me. "Can I paint a dog into the scene? Maybe with a ball?"

"Honey, you can do whatever you want with it, and I'll proudly display it. What do I owe you?"

She nibbles her bottom lip. "Tanner would roll his eyes at me right now because he's an art dealer, but honestly, I don't want you to pay me for it."

"Absolutely, not. Your husband is right, you don't work for free."

"But sometimes, I do. It can't all be work. There has to be some art that I do just for fun, because it feels good. Otherwise, I'll burn out on it. So, since you're giving me so much artistic rein, I won't charge you for it."

"I don't feel right about that," I reply, shaking my head. "I want to pay you."

"Let's work out a trade," she suggests. "I don't know what that is yet, but we'll figure it out."

"Deal."

We shake hands on it, and then the front door opens, and Cherry walks in carrying a basket of laundry.

She stops short when she sees us at the window, and her eyes drop to where I'm still holding Sarah's hand.

"I, uh, I'm sorry if I interrupted something."

Jesus, does she think that I'd romance a *married woman*?

"Sarah's going to paint me something for the wall," I reply, but the suspicion doesn't leave Cherry's eyes.

"He's letting me paint pretty much whatever I want," Sarah adds with a grin. "For over the sofa."

Sarah's phone rings in her pocket, and she immediately pulls it out and answers.

"Hey, sweetheart. Yeah, I'm almost done here at Zeke's. This painting is going to rock. Sure, I can do that. Okay, see you soon. Love you, too."

As she talks, I don't take my eyes off Cherry, who's still frowning and decide here and now to have a talk with her when Sarah leaves.

"I'd better go, I have to stop by the store to get some butter for whatever Tanner's making for dinner. If butter's involved, I want it," Sarah says and takes a minute to look between Cherry and me, a knowing smile on her pretty face. "Thanks again for letting me do this. I promise it's gonna rock. But, if you hate it, we don't have to hang it."

"I won't hate it," I assure her as I walk her to the door, past Cherry, who's stepped aside. "It's going to be awesome. Have a good night."

"You, too. Bye, Cherry."

"See you," Cherry says as I close the door behind Sarah. Then, I turn to Cherry with a scowl.

"What the hell is wrong with you?"

Chapter Three

Cherry

"What's wrong with *me*?" I set the basket of clothes on the floor, good and pissed off now, even if it *is* irrational. I saw him holding Sarah's hand, and I just saw red. I wanted to punch them both, and that's not like me. But I just couldn't help myself. "What do you mean, what's wrong with me?"

"You were rude to her, and for no reason at all. I mean, I'm used to that when it's directed at *me*, but not Sarah. She's your friend."

The jealousy still sits like bile in the back of my throat. I hope I wasn't rude to Sarah. I *like* the woman.

"I wasn't rude to her. I didn't say anything at all *rude*."

"You don't have a poker face, sweetheart. And from the look of it you thought I'd try to diddle with a married woman, and that's insulting to both Sarah *and* me."

"Those words never left my lips."

But, I admit, for about three seconds, I did think it. And that's just ridiculous because Sarah is madly in love with Tanner. Has been since we were in high school.

I know better. And, yes, I need to apologize to him, but I just can't get the words past my lips.

He shakes his head in frustration, and I lift the basket and head for the door.

"I'll use my parents' house from now on. I'm sorry to be in your way."

"For fuck's sake," he mutters and rushes toward me, planting his hand on the door and pushing it closed when I've managed to open it just a few inches. "You're the most frustrating woman I've ever met in my goddamn life."

"Then why do you want me here?" I demand and turn to face him, shoving him back so I can breathe because having him so close makes my brain foggy. "And that's not a rhetorical question, because even *I* wouldn't want me around when I'm acting this way. If I'm always a bitch, and I make you so mad, just let me go to my parents' house. You'll never have to speak to me again."

"Because that sounds like a fucking prison sentence," he shouts back. "Because I *like* having you here, and I hate it all at the same time. Which I know sounds stupid, but there it is."

"We make each other nuts," I remind him. "And I'm a nag. Not to mention, rude to your friends."

"Exactly." He throws his hands up into the air and paces away. "So, why do I want you so badly that I ache with it? Why do I want to fuck you into next week, make you laugh, and just sit and *talk* to you for hours?"

That stuns me into silence. Certain I heard him wrong, all I can do is blink at him until he turns to look at me once more.

"Why did you act that way?"

"Because I was jealous." The words are out of my mouth faster than I can stop them, and his eyes soften as his shoulders fall. I know that we're through the worst of this argument. Which is good because I don't enjoy sparring with Zeke the way I used to. Something has changed between us, and I'm so far out of my element with him, I feel like I'm fumbling my way through the dark. "And I know that's stupid, and I have no right because you can do whatever the hell you want, with whomever you want, but when I walked in here and saw you standing all cozy by the windows, holding some broad's hand, I was jealous. And then I realized that it was Sarah."

"Why were you jealous, Cherry?"

His voice has deepened, and he's slowly walking toward me, every line in his impressive body taut with energy.

"I—" I have to lick my lips as he moves even closer. "Don't know."

He's just a foot away from me now and reaches up to gently glide his knuckles over the apple of my cheek. I feel that simple touch in every nerve of my body.

"Did the thought of me touching someone else like this make you uncomfortable?"

I frown because I don't want to admit that it made me *more* than uncomfortable. It made me angry.

It made me a smidge homicidal.

"Something like that."

Zeke takes the basket I'm still holding out of my hands, sets it on the floor, and then leans into me even more.

"I can't think straight when you're this close to me," I admit softly.

"Good."

He presses my back against the door and kisses me, just the way he did the other night at my condo, like he's starved for me. His hands wander down my arms, up the sides of my torso, and then down again to rest on my hips as his mouth does things to me that I've only seen in the movies.

And I'm no virgin.

My hand lands on his chest, but it's not to push him away. It's to anchor myself. I need something to hold on to, and right now, that's Zeke.

"You're the sexiest woman I've ever seen," he murmurs before placing little kisses on my cheeks and finally my forehead. "I don't want to fight with you anymore, Cherry."

"Okay." I swallow hard, still in the fuzzy haze of that kiss. "No more fighting."

"I want to turn this around with you. *Date* you."

That has my eyes springing open in surprise.

"You thought I was going to say fuck you."

"I, well, yeah. I did."

His lips turn up in that arrogant smile he has that used to piss me off. Now, it doesn't irritate me so badly. "Trust me, I want that, too, but that's not all I want."

"Why?"

That question has him blinking in surprise and taking a step back to push his hand through his hair as he thinks about his answer.

"You're a beautiful woman, but you already know that."

"I'm okay. Beauty's in the eye of the beholder."

"Always have to argue," he mutters, shaking his head, but he's smiling rather than scowling at me. "I'm the beholder, and I say you're hot."

"Okay."

"But it's more than that." He begins pacing like he's totally agitated and confused, and I have to admit, it's fascinating to watch. "Because I *like* your sassy mouth, and I want to get to know you better. So, yeah, I want to fuck you, and I want to take you out so I can have conversations with you."

"We can have conversations here."

"No." He shakes his head, clearly against the idea. "No. If we hang out here to talk, I'll just get you naked. If we're in public, the odds of that are much lower."

"So, you *don't* want to see me naked?"

"No, I definitely want to see you naked. A lot. All the time, in fact."

"I'm so confused."

Zeke laughs and tips his head back to stare at the ceiling. "I am, too."

I cross my arms over my chest and can't help but smile at him. "So, are you saying that you don't want to have sex until after we get to know each other better? Because that's a little...old-fashioned."

"I definitely didn't say that." He shakes his head. "I guess I'm just telling you that I don't want to just hit it and leave. It won't be a one-time deal for me."

"What if it's bad?"

That makes his eyes smolder again. "It's not going to be bad. I can guarantee you that."

I raise an eyebrow. "Wow. Sure of yourself, aren't you?"

He moves in on me again, and I don't plant my hand on his chest to stop him. I don't do anything at all. I just wait to see what his next move will be.

I let out a yelp when he simply lifts me onto his shoulder and carries me caveman-style back to his bedroom.

Zeke tosses me onto the bed and quickly crawls over me, pinning me beneath him, then goes right back to kissing me.

The man obviously loves to kiss, and I'm not about to complain about it because he's damn good at it. And I know the sex will be good, too. I just can't stop teasing him. It's like it's my third job or something.

"Cherry," he murmurs next to my ear.

"Mm-hmm?"

"Tell me now if this isn't what you want. No hard feelings."

"If you stop, I might set your house on fire, which would be sad because I like this place."

I feel him smile against my neck, and it sends a shiver of anticipation down to my belly.

I expect him to move fast, to strip us down quickly, and just go for it. But he doesn't.

He leisurely tugs my shirt over my head and then settles in to gently touch and kiss what feels like every square inch of my torso before pulling the clasp of my bra free and exposing my breasts.

Zeke sighs before dipping his head and taking an already hard nipple into his mouth.

"Oh, damn," I mutter, arching my back. My body is on *fire*. I've never felt this kind of need running through me for a man before. Like if he stops touching me, I'll combust from the heat of it. "Please, Zeke."

"What, baby?" He nibbles down to my navel. "What do you need?"

"Faster." My legs scissor, my core needing release. "Move *faster*."

That's all he needs to hear because he's suddenly sliding my jeans down my legs, followed by my underwear. As I lie before him, naked as the day I was born, he sits up to hastily strip out of his own clothes and toss them aside.

"Wait." I lay my hand on his arm, slowing him down for just a moment. "I don't want to stop, but I want to...look at you."

His eyes narrow on mine, and then I lazily let my gaze wander over his tanned skin, down his flat stomach—perfectly chiseled—and lower still to where his hard erection waits for me.

"You're a stunning man, Zeke."

"You're fucking killing me here, baby."

"Well, I don't know what in the world you're waiting for."

He laughs and leans down to bite my shoulder, then reaches to the bedside table and retrieves a condom.

After rolling on the protection, he doesn't immediately push inside me.

Instead, he nudges his way between my legs and reaches down to massage and drive me out of my mind with his magical fingers.

"So damn wet," he growls.

"You're doing things to me. Of course, I'm wet," I reply and then bite my lip when, with two fingers inside me, he plants his thumb on my clit and sends me into the stratosphere.

"Damn." He kisses my lips softly. "So damn responsive."

"Zeke?"

"Yeah?"

"If you don't fuck me in three seconds—"

Before I can finish the thought, he pushes inside me, stretching me to accommodate him, and my hands immediately grip the sheets tightly.

"Me," he says. "Grab onto *me*, Cherry. Not the bed."

So, I do. My hands clasp onto his back, run down to his ass, and I'm not at all worried that I'm likely leaving marks with my nails. I just need to *hold on* as he takes me on the most amazing ride.

His body moves so gracefully as he pushes and pulls in a steady rhythm that has us both breathing hard and moaning.

Finally, I can't hold back the second orgasm already rolling through me, and as I contract around him, Zeke follows me over the edge, succumbing to his release.

He collapses on top of me, panting and sweating, until I finally push on his shoulder.

"Can't breathe."

"Sorry." He manages to roll to the side, still fighting to catch his breath.

"It didn't suck."

"Huh?" He looks my way.

"You were right, it didn't suck."

He chuckles and turns onto his side so he's facing me. "Told you. It couldn't be bad. I'm too fucking into you."

"Are you a masochist?" I sit up and reach for a throw blanket to cover myself with. "Because I haven't been the nicest to you."

"I probably am. Haven't been before, but I guess there's a first time for everything."

He sits and faces me, seemingly not at all interested in covering himself.

"But I'll tell you this," he continues, "I'm not a submissive."

"Thank God." I giggle at that. "I can't picture you letting anyone dominate you."

"I don't know, I've put up with a lot from you over the past year."

I narrow my eyes at him. "You had it coming."

"Sometimes," he concedes and reaches out to push his fingers through my hair. "Sometimes, I did something to get a rise out of you because it was the only way you'd give me the time of day."

"You could have tried being *nice*. We might have ended up here sooner."

He pulls me in for a kiss and then winks. "Where's the fun in that?"

Chapter Four

Zeke

"What is that?"

Cherry opens one bleary eye and stares at the mug in my hand. I managed to talk her into staying the night with me, and I have to admit, I liked it.

"Coffee."

She frowns and stretches between the sheets, then sighs.

"I don't drink coffee."

I scowl down at her. "I'm sorry, I think I misheard you."

Her bee-stung lips tip up in a sleepy smile. "I can't stand coffee."

"Like, at all?"

"Nope."

"Are you an alien?"

"Yep."

I stare down into the mug, then shrug and take a sip. "More for me, then. How'd you sleep?"

"Like the dead. I don't think I moved all night. I should exercise before bed more often."

"If I have my say, you will be." I take another sip and reach out to rub her thigh. "What do you have on the docket today?"

"Making candles," she replies with a sigh. "I have two hundred to get done for a special order."

"Holy shit, two *hundred* candles? On your day off?"

"I don't have days off, Zeke." She shakes her head and then ruffles her hair, scratching her scalp. "But that's okay. I have bills to pay, and this order was huge. In fact, what time is it?"

"Just past eight."

"I should get home and get started on it. Do you mind if I start a load of laundry on my way out? I never got to it last night."

I can't help it. I lean in and kiss her softly. "I don't mind."

"Thanks." She's holding the throw against her and just looks at me. "What?"

"I need you to leave so I can get out of your bed and get dressed."

I cock my head to the side. "Why do you need me to leave for that?"

"Because I'm *naked.*"

I don't move a fucking muscle. "I hate to break it to you, but I've already seen everything you have to offer."

"That's different."

"Why?"

"Because it was while we had sex."

Narrowing my eyes, I take another sip of the coffee. "So, if I see you naked when we're *not* having sex, that's not okay?"

"When you put it like that, it sounds stupid. But, yes."

"Why?"

"I don't have time for this conversation."

She moves to get out of bed, taking the blanket with her, but I quickly set the mug aside and cover her, pinning her beneath me.

"There will never be a day, in this or any other lifetime, that you need to be shy about your body with me, Cherry. Or with anything, for that matter."

"I'm not *shy.*"

She twists her lips together, so I lean in and kiss her once more. "Okay. I'll go."

"Thanks," she whispers as I stand. Then, taking my coffee with me, I leave the bedroom.

The dynamic of our relationship has completely changed in the span of less than a week. Instead of being annoyed by the simple sight of her, or the mention of her name, I suddenly want to be near her constantly.

And the sex? Out of this fucking world.

I'm surprised the smoke alarms didn't go off.

I've just finished my coffee and set the mug in the dishwasher when Cherry walks out of my bedroom and retrieves her basket from where we left it last night, then disappears again down the hall and into the laundry room.

I hear the washer start, and then she's back, now dressed but her hair still askew.

"What can I have on hand for you for the mornings since you don't like coffee?"

"Oh, you don't—"

"Okay, that's fucking annoying."

She frowns, and I grab a rag to wipe down the countertop.

"I know I don't *have* to do anything. But I want to, and I plan to have more nights with you. You must drink something in the morning. What is it?"

"Green tea," she says. "With honey."

"Milk?"

"No, just the honey."

"I can do that. See, that wasn't so hard, was it?"

"Everything with you is hard," she mumbles and then rolls her eyes when I smile smugly. "Not *that*, perv."

"Oh, yeah. *That*." She reaches for the front door. "Stop."

She turns, one eyebrow raised.

"I'm gonna need a kiss."

"You've had a million of them."

"One more."

I lean my hip against the counter, waiting for her to come to me. After just one second of thought, she walks over to me, boosts onto her tiptoes, and puckers up.

I oblige her, leaning down to meet her, pressing my lips to her soft ones. She pulls away quickly to march back to the door.

"See you later," she says as she opens it.

"Count on it."

* * * *

"You brought me lunch?"

Five hours later, I'm standing at the threshold of Cherry's condo, holding a paper bag full of subs and chips. She's dressed in little shorts, a tank top, and nothing else.

Even her hair is up in a messy bun thing on top of her head, exposing the long line of her neck, and it conjures the need to nibble that irresistible skin.

"You're a goddamn goddess."

"Right." She rolls her eyes, but I also see the faint blush on her cheeks. "Is that lunch?"

"Oh, yeah. Sandwiches. Thought you'd need food by now. And maybe some help, too."

"Are you the help?"

"I'm the only one standing here."

"Okay, come in." She steps back, gesturing for me to come inside, and then closes the door behind me. "I need a quick break anyway."

"How many have you made so far? I take it the scent of them is lavender, given that your condo smells like lavender fields."

"You'd be right. I'm about fifty in."

I blink at her as she pulls the food out of the bag. "Only fifty?"

"That's a lot, actually."

"Jesus, you'll be doing this well into the night."

"That's the plan." She unwraps a sub. "Which one is mine?"

"They're both the same. Turkey."

"Cool." She takes a big bite and reaches for a napkin to wipe the mayonnaise off her lip. "It's a process of making sure the wax is the correct temperature, adding the scent and color dye, pouring, placing wicks, labeling the jars."

"I can help. Seriously, I don't have any other plans today. I can label jars and place wicks or whatever."

She eyes me for a moment, chewing on her turkey sandwich, and then nods.

"I'll happily put you to work, and I'll even loan you an apron."

I eye her as I chew my own sandwich. "You're not wearing an apron."

"I took it off a minute ago when I went to the restroom. Trust me, the wax can splash. The apron will save your clothes and a potential burn."

"You've sold me on the apron. Will it be pink and frilly?"

"Sorry, the only one I have is red." She laughs as she finishes half her sub, then wraps the other half and stows it in the fridge for later. She offers me a soda, and we're comfortably quiet as we finish our lunch.

When my sandwich is gone, I toss the wrapper away and follow her into her guest bedroom.

"Whoa."

The room isn't set up for guests. Instead, she has big tables against three of the walls. A large cabinet dominates the wall with the door, and above the tables are shelves for more storage. There are even cabinets and totes *under* the tables for additional storage space.

I see some big slow-cooker-looking things with spigots on the front on one end. And dozens of jars set on the tables, some full, others waiting to be filled.

"Whoa," I say again, and Cherry grins back at me.

"Yeah, this is the craft room. This is where I daydream and create pretty things."

"What else do you make besides candles?"

She adds some white flakes to the slow cooker, which I assume is wax.

"I do wax melts, room sprays, shower sprays, bath bombs, salves. You name it, I can probably make it."

"So, which one is your passion?"

She frowns over at me and blows a stray lock of hair out of her eyes. I cross to her to hook that strand behind her ear.

"What do you mean?"

"Just what I asked. Is the crafting or the teaching what you're passionate about?"

"Oh, the crafts for sure." She gets back to work, pulling supplies out of drawers. "I mean, don't get me wrong, I like the kids. Well, most of the time. Sometimes, it's a slog to get through the day, but all in all, it's not bad. But this? My online store? That's what I really love to do. I like coming up with new things, new scents, learning about how different oils work together for healing. I think it's fascinating and a lot of fun. The store does pretty well, but it would probably do better if I could devote more time to it."

"Why don't you?"

She smirks, shaking her head. "Because going into business for yourself full time is a gamble that I can't afford to take. If it fails, I'm fucked. I don't come from a wealthy family that can bail me out if something goes wrong. It's just me, and the thought of being even more trapped than I already am is not something I want to ever happen. It just can't."

"But it could also do amazing," I insist. "Sure, it *could* fail, but the chances are just as good, or better, that you could not only make a good living but excel at it. You could sell your products locally, in stores."

"You sound like Montana," she says with a chuckle. "She's always saying the same thing. 'Sell at farmer's markets, consign at some of the shops.'"

"I don't think that sounds like a bad idea at all."

"It's too iffy." She blows out a breath. "I need stability in my life, and working for someone else, for a set number of hours, knowing how much my paychecks will be, that's stability."

"But do you *love* it?"

"I love the assurance that I'm not broke." She turns to me with the apron. "Now, let's change the subject. Here's your apron."

"Will you tie it on?"

She grins and crosses to me, slipping the loop over my head before reaching around to tie the strings in the back. Her eyes are on mine as her breasts press to my belly, and I feel my blood get hot.

"I don't have time for any shenanigans," she warns me.

"I didn't say anything."

"You didn't have to. You don't have a poker face either."

Cherry smirks and then turns to the business at hand.

"Okay, this will be a twenty-jar batch. Are you ready?"

"As I'll ever be. Just tell me what to do."

She's an excellent teacher. Patient and ready to explain everything step by step, as we move through all twenty jars.

I'm surprised by how complicated the process is.

"You know, I've never given much thought to how candles are made It's not easy."

"Eh, it's not *hard*. You just need to have the math down."

"Yeah, I don't do math."

"Sure, you do. You work on cars."

"That's not math."

"It's a *lot* of math, you just don't know it." She grins over at me, and want to kiss her.

Again.

She makes me feel smart and sexy and just *good* whenever I'm with her.

Why did it take me so long to see that?

"Zeke?"

"Yeah?"

"Would you like to take a turn pouring?"

"Oh, sure. Whatever you need. Where should we start?"

"First, we need to label the jars and set the wicks. Then we pour when the wax is up to temperature, and we've added the scent."

"I feel like I should be paying you for this class."

"Oh, this one's free. The next one, though, that'll cost you."

Chapter Five

Cherry

I feel like I owe him.

I know that Zeke would roll his eyes at that and probably tell me not to think twice about it, but the man helped me for hours and hours over the weekend to get those candles finished and shipped out. He refused to leave until everything was done, boxed, labeled, and then cleaned up.

He worked his butt off, right beside me.

And I have to admit, I had a great time, which was a huge surprise because this is *Zeke* we're talking about.

Except, he doesn't drive me bonkers like he used to. In fact, he hardly makes me want to smother him with a pillow at all anymore.

Instead, I'd rather hold on tightly to that pillow while he does all kinds of delicious things to my body. And he doesn't seem to want to stop doing that anytime soon.

Thank all the gods and goddesses.

Still, I wanted to do something nice to thank Zeke for all his hard work and help, so here I am at Wolfe's Garage at closing time, showing up to surprise him.

When I walk into the garage, classic rock 'n' roll pounds out of the speakers, and a pair of legs sticks out of the underside of a truck, a toe tapping the air to the beat of the song.

There doesn't seem to be anyone else here, so I walk over to the legs squat down, and bend like a pretzel to look under the truck to see who I'm interrupting.

It's Zeke.

The music is so loud, and he's so absorbed in what he's doing that he doesn't see me.

"Boo!"

He jumps, hits his head on the underside of the truck, and then quickly rolls out from under it, rubbing his forehead and scowling at me.

I've fallen back on my ass, laughing like a damn loon.

"You can't just sneak up on a guy like that." He's still rubbing the spot. "Siri, stop the music."

We're suddenly cast in complete silence, aside from my laughter.

"I'm sorry, but that music was so loud, you wouldn't have heard me if I knocked or something."

"Have you ever heard of a phone?"

"Here." I scoot to him and move his hand out of the way so I can rub his forehead. "I'm sorry you hurt yourself. Do you have a concussion?"

"No, just a bump."

I boost up onto my knees so I can kiss the small red spot. He wraps his arms around my waist and tugs me into his lap, still sitting on the rolly thing, and plants his lips on mine for a long, hard kiss.

"Feel better?" I ask when I come up for air.

"Somewhat. To what do I owe this visit? Or did you just stop by to try to decapitate me?"

"You're so dramatic. It's closing time, and I have a surprise for you."

He lifts an eyebrow in interest. "Really? What is it?"

"Finish up what you're doing here so I can show you."

He kisses my cheek, moves me off his lap so he can stand, then pulls me onto my feet with him. It only takes him about ten minutes to get everything put away and closed down for the night, and then we walk out to my car.

"To thank you for all your hard work over the weekend, I'm taking you on a picnic."

"I'm *starving*."

"Good, because I have a ton of food. Get in."

The drive to the beach access I want to take Zeke to isn't far from the garage, and soon I've parked and have the back hatch open to retrieve the picnic basket I loaded down.

Zeke takes it from me and frowns. "This is fucking heavy."

"I told you, I brought a lot of food."

Rather than hit the button to close the hatch, I reach up to do it manually and carry the blanket I brought for us to sit on.

"I know we have beach access at the condos," I begin as we descend the stairs to the sand below, "but it's nice to shake things up sometimes."

"Couldn't agree more."

When we're settled with the blanket spread out and the basket open, we just sit for a minute to take in the view of the water and the amazingly calm breeze.

"You'd never know it was November today." I pull some cheese out of the basket. "It feels like early fall, so I figured we'd take advantage of it. Although, there is a slight nip of chill on the air."

"I like it," he says with a shrug. "My dad was stationed in really hot places quite a bit, so I like the cooler weather."

"Your dad was military?"

I have a plate of meats and cheeses, along with olives, pickled veggies, crackers, and spreads, and we begin digging into the food.

"Army," Zeke confirms around a bite of salami. "Career Army. He was a lieutenant colonel when he retired and was well-liked and respected."

"Was he strict?"

"Oh, yeah. But not in a mean or heavy-handed way. I just always knew what he expected of me and didn't really put up much of a fight because he was gone a lot, and it was just me and my mom. My mom is kick-ass, so doing my share around the house never bothered me."

"Are you still close to them?" I love hearing about Zeke's childhood and his relationship with his parents.

"Sure. We talk about once a week. I'm trying to convince them to come here for the holidays, but we'll see. Mom's afraid to fly, and they've been living in Virginia since Dad retired."

"That would be a long drive," I agree with a nod.

"What about you?"

"I don't mind flying."

He grins and reaches out to playfully tug on a piece of my hair.

"Are you close to your parents?"

I pop a sprig of pickled asparagus into my mouth, thinking about m answer. "I love them, sure. Am I *close* to them? Not really. Though not in a bad way. I just don't see them often."

"Where do they live?"

"Here in town." He lifts an eyebrow, and I shrug in response. "It was a...different kind of childhood."

"In what way?"

I blow out a breath and watch the water roll and churn with the waves beating on the sand. When I was young, I sometimes thought I was the sand, and life was those waves, because it always felt like I could never catch a break.

"Okay, so, I'm not looking for sympathy here. This is just how it was."

"Got it." He nods, listening.

"My family was really poor. Like, *really* poor. My parents were never going to send me to college, buy me my first car, or help me get my first house. They couldn't pay for their own life, let alone even think about helping me with mine. Which is totally fine. I don't need the help, I'm just explaining."

"I understand," he says, still nodding and chewing.

"They never tried to hide the fact that they were broke to me. I knew when the electricity went out, it likely wasn't because of a storm, it was because they couldn't pay the bill. We used food banks and pantries, and I never had new clothes. In fact, shopping for *new* school clothes meant making a trip to the thrift store. But my mom always tried to sew what we bought in different ways so that it was new for *me*. Does that make sense?"

"Sure."

There's no judgment at all on his face, no censure or disgust, and I feel perfectly safe confiding in him.

"One time, when I was in the fifth grade, I went to school, and a little girl who doesn't live here anymore pointed at my new-to-me shirt and said, 'That was mine!' I was so fucking embarrassed. I went home crying, and my mom swore she'd do better to make the clothes look different. She was great with a sewing machine. Anyway, we depended on the goodwill of others a lot."

"Were your parents unable to work?"

"They worked, but I think they were in this horrible cycle of not making much money, and something *always* came up. The car would break down, or taxes would come due. Always *something*. I can't even tell you how many times we had to move in the middle of the night because they couldn't pay the rent, and we had to skip out on the landlords."

"That must be hard to do in Huckleberry Bay. It's a tiny town."

"For sure. I think people knew their circumstances and didn't try very hard to get their money out of them. Maybe because they had me, I don't know. And I also have to say, my parents are good people. They never hurt me, neglected me, or abused me. I felt loved, and we laughed a lot. But it also instilled in me some anxiety about being poor. I will *not* live like that ever again, so I'm pretty frugal. Montana says I'm an old lady about a lot of things, but—"

"But you had to be the adult," he finishes for me.

"Yeah. I got a job when I was fourteen, and I've worked ever since. That helped my parents a lot because I was able to pay some of the bills."

Now, his jaw hardens. "You paid the bills as a teenager?"

"Some of them. We didn't lose electricity again or have to move in the middle of the night. So, I was happy to do it."

Now that we're finished eating, I pack up the empty plates and used napkins and close the basket.

"I guess that was a really long-winded way to answer your question. I don't have any ill will toward my parents, but they're still stuck in that same rut of poverty, and I just can't do it. I can't live like that, and I can't watch them do it either because they spend money poorly and make bad life choices."

"Do they ask you for money? Now that you're an adult?"

"They used to. When I first moved out of the house, they thought I'd continue paying the bills that I paid when I lived with them. But I couldn't because I had my own bills to pay. I had to set some hard boundaries and splurged on some therapy to help me out in that area."

"I don't think that was a splurge. I think it was a necessity."

I nod in agreement. "You're right. We love each other, and I'm always happy when I run into them, but we don't seek each other out like other families do. I think it makes them uncomfortable."

"And that's why you need the stability."

"That's why."

Zeke reaches out and takes my hand in his, rubbing his thumb over my knuckles. "Thanks for sharing all of that with me."

"Ready to run for the hills?"

"Not even close." He leans in and kisses me softly. "I have a request. Well, that's not entirely true. I'd like to invite you out on a date."

"We're on a date."

"A different date," he says with a grin. "There's a gala happening for the Huckleberry Bay Chamber of Commerce, and because I'm a business owner, I'm supposed to go. I wasn't going to, but now that I have a hot date, it might be fun."

I know that gala. The city has been putting it on for as long as I can remember, and I never thought in a million years I'd be asked to go.

"When is it?"

"Next weekend."

I feel my eyes go wide.

"If you don't want to go—"

"No, it's not that. I just don't have anything to wear. But Montana might have something she can loan me. She's gone before."

"Is that a yes?"

I smile over at him. "You sure you want to be seen with me in public since all we've done before is fight in front of everyone?"

"It'll just be proof of my charming ways that I got you to come around."

The laugh that spills out of me is loud and full of humor. "Right. That's it for sure. What the hell, I'll go with you."

"Good. Now, let's take a walk on this beach."

"Let's go."

* * * *

"I need your help."

Montana looks up from the ice cream counter where she's taking notes on a pad, and her eyes widen.

"Are you okay? Are you running from the law?"

That makes me stop short. "Jesus, no."

"Just making sure I don't have to drive the getaway car or something. Okay, what's up?"

"You know the chamber of commerce gala next week?"

"Yeah?"

"I'm going."

Now, she just blinks at me in surprise. "With whom? I asked you to go as my date and you turned me down."

"Don't get whiny. Zeke asked me."

More blinking.

"I thought you hated Zeke and the ground he walks on."

"Well." I cringe and move from one foot to the other. "I did. But we've started sleeping together and—"

"WHAT?" Montana flails her arms in the air, stopping me. "Hold up, Cherry Pomegranate Dubois."

"I hate my middle name."

"Back that shit right up, right now. You know what? Hold on."

Montana stomps to the front door and locks it, flipping the open sign to closed, then marches back over to me, takes my hand, and drags me to a nearby table, forcing me into a chair.

"I've been your best friend since the third grade."

"True."

"And now you're fucking a hot mechanic, and you didn't think that was information you should share with your life-long bestie?"

"Don't be mad." I sigh and sit back in the chair. "It happened really, really fast."

"Uh, yeah. Because at the Halloween party, you hated each other."

My lips twitch. "It all started later that night, actually."

Montana listens intently as I run through everything from the first cold shower to earlier on the beach. When I've finished, she simply stares at me.

"Say something."

"Who are you and what have you done with my best friend?"

I roll my eyes at her. "Stop it. I'm just having some fun with him, that's all. And I have to take a shower and wash my clothes somewhere. He was nice enough to offer to help me."

"Uh-huh. I mean, you could put up with some bad sex in exchange for hot water privileges."

"Ew. We're not *trading services*, Monty. Gross."

"You *like him*." She stabs a finger in my direction. "Admit it."

"I like him." I sigh and scrub my hands over my face. "Like, *really* like him, and that shocks me more than anybody else. Also? He's started turning his music off early, and he doesn't park like an asshole anymore. It's like he's *trying* to stay on my good side."

Now, Montana busts up laughing. "Well, duh. He wants to continue getting in your pants. He's not going to try to piss you off."

"I like him," I repeat.

"Why does that make you look sad?"

"Because it's been my experience that when I like a guy, they end up disappointing me. But I guess I'll just ride the wave until it ends, right?"

"You're such an optimist."

"But am I wrong?"

"No, you're not wrong."

"Back to my original question. Do you have something I can wear? You've been going to this thing for a long time."

"Of course, I do. In fact, I have a black number that will make Zeke weep tears of mercy."

"Good. Let's go with that one."

Chapter Six

Zeke

"Not that I'm trying to get you out of my place, quite the contrary really, but when are you getting your water heater fixed?"

Cherry and I are in my bathroom, both of us getting ready for tonight's gala. Thankfully, I have a few suits that I've worn in recent years for other fancy parties, and Cherry helped me choose a black one with a blue shirt.

She says it'll match her dress, but she hasn't let me get a look at said dress yet.

It's killing me.

"I don't have plans to have it fixed."

I stop, my razor halfway down my face, and stare at her in the mirror as she applies something pink to her cheek.

"What?"

She doesn't spare me a glance.

"I haven't scheduled it."

"Why not?"

Cherry shrugs one terrycloth-clad shoulder. "Because I can't afford a new hot water heater right now, and I'm getting by without it, so it's not on my priority list."

Her eyes meet mine then.

"But if you're sick of sharing with me, I'll figure something else out."

"I didn't say that. I was just wondering about the water heater. You can shower here until the end of time. I don't mind at all. But shit, Cherry, you need to have it fixed."

"I will. Eventually."

"Let me—"

"No." She shakes her head and drops a brush into her bag. "Absolutely, not."

"You can pay me back. It's not charity, it's a necessity."

"Not right now, it isn't," she murmurs.

"Look, I'm not trying to pry into your private financial business, but you just sold two hundred candles in one swoop."

"That money isn't for the heater, it's for other things."

I love that Cherry's financially responsible because those values align with mine, and I know we won't have issues in this area, but this seems unreasonable even to me.

"Drop it," she says before I can continue. "It'll get fixed when I can do it. I don't mean to be a bitch about it, but I've got it handled."

"Okay. If you say so."

"Now, I'm going into the guest bedroom so I can get dressed."

She's done her hair into a pretty twisty knot thing, and her makeup is perfect, setting off those gorgeous round eyes and plump lips.

"We could just stay here, and you can get naked," I suggest, reaching for her, but she dodges out of my way and laughs.

"No way, I put too much work into this. I'll be out in a few."

I finish shaving and dress in the suit, only getting hung up on tying the tie once.

I fucking hate ties.

Just when I've put the finishing touches on styling my hair, I sense movement behind me. When I turn, I just about swallow my tongue.

Fucking hell, she's gorgeous in a long, sleek black dress that exposes one shoulder and hugs her breasts and hips *perfectly*.

It's loose around her feet, and I can't help but lean down to raise the hem so I can get a peek at her heels.

"I didn't realize you're a shoe man."

"When they look like that, hell, yes, I am. Jesus, baby, you're absolutely gorgeous."

"So are you." She reaches out to straighten my tie, and I can't help but lean in to kiss her, careful not to mess up her makeup.

"I'm going to be arrested before the night is over."

She frowns. "Why?"

"Because I'm going to have to kill every man there for looking at you and thinking what I am right now."

"What are you thinking?"

"How I can't wait to get you out of this dress later."

She smirks, but I shake my head.

"Dead serious. You're beautiful, sweetheart."

"Thanks. Let's go before we're late."

* * * *

"I'm nervous," Cherry whispers to me as we walk into the ballroom where the HBCOC is holding the gala.

"Are you kidding me? Honey, looking the way you do, you're about to own that room."

She smiles gratefully, but it's the absolute truth.

The chamber president meets us at the door and gives instructions for where to find our table and when dinner will be served.

And then, when we get fully inside, I hear Cherry breathe a huge sigh of relief. My gaze follows hers, and I see Montana, the owner of the ice cream shop in town, Huckleberry Delight.

"You're here," Montana says with a big grin, hugging Cherry hard when we reach her. "Girl, you look better in that dress than I ever did."

"I know, right?" Cherry says with a laugh and does a little twirl.

Another hand-me-down dress. Knowing what I do about Cherry's childhood, I'm going to do everything in my power to ensure that this is the last used piece of clothing she wears.

"We're at the same table," Montana continues, leading us to a round table right in the middle of the room. "With Luna and Wolfe and Sarah and Tanner."

"And Indigo Lovejoy," Cherry adds, giving Montana a look. "He's sitting next to you."

"Yep." Montana doesn't look happy about that.

"You okay?" Cherry asks.

"It's fine."

"Indigo is a great guy," I say, speaking for the first time. Both pairs of female eyes turn to me, and I shrug. "Well, he is. He's my friend."

"He's a nice guy," Montana says, nodding slowly. "I won't argue with that. Anyway, this should be fun. There's a silent auction with the proceeds going to Samson House."

"Oh, I love that."

"What's Samson House?" I ask.

"That's right, you're still pretty new here," Montana replies with a kind smile. "It's a shelter that helps people out, and they're fabulous. The food pantry is one of the best on the west coast, and they even keep storage facilities to store furniture and household goods so when people get back on their feet, they have something to start with. No charge."

"That's incredible."

"They really are," Cherry agrees. "I'm so glad they'll be receiving some money from this. I'll have to check out the auction."

"You do that. I'm going to freshen up in the little girls' room," Montana says. "I'll catch up with you in a few."

With my hand on the small of Cherry's back, we make our way to the edge of the room, which is lined with tables displaying all kinds of things up for auction. They even included a painting done by Sarah, which already has half a page of bids and is currently going for well into the four figures.

"Oh, look at these," Cherry says, fingering a pair of dangling silver earrings. "They're so pretty."

She'll have them by the time the night is over.

We browse, pausing here and there to get a better look. A waiter comes by with champagne, and we both take a glass.

So far, it's a pleasant, laid-back evening, and the looks coming Cherry's way haven't been lost on me.

We're admiring a sculpture made of driftwood when a man speaks next to Cherry, not to her but loud enough for us to hear him.

"I can't believe we're going to spend all this money just for it to go to some homeless shelter. Aren't there better places for it to go? Those people need to get a job and stop leaching off those of us who aren't afraid of a hard days' work."

Cherry stiffens beside me, but I clasp her hand in mine as we continue to listen.

"I mean, Jesus, there has to be more than fifty-thousand dollars here, all for a homeless shelter? How much toothpaste do they need?"

"I don't know," I say, cutting in and grabbing his attention. "I guess I'd rather be poor and ask for help than be an asshole."

I smile widely, and I can tell the other man doesn't know whether I'm joking or not.

And we don't stick around for him to find out. If I stay, I'll end up punching him in his ugly, pompous face.

Instead, Cherry and I walk to the table where everyone else is already seated.

"I can't believe you just said that," Cherry says, laughing so hard she has to wipe a tear from her eye. "Zeke essentially just called Harley Anderson an asshole."

"The rich jerk who has a perpetual scowl on his old, wrinkled face?" Indigo asks, looking around the room. "He *is* an asshole."

"So, Sarah told me that I wasn't allowed to ask questions tonight," Tanner begins, shaking his head. "But I'm going to anyway because it was less than a month ago that I thought the two of you were going to break out in a fistfight at Annabelle's party. So, what happened?"

"My water heater busted," Cherry replies smoothly. "And he wasn't a jerk about it."

"I feel like we're missing a *huge* part of that story," Luna says, glaring daggers at Wolfe. "You haven't even filled *me* in on this, and you had to know."

"Not my story to tell," Wolfe replies with a shrug.

"So, no more hate, and now you're dating?" Indigo asks, clearly avoiding any contact with Montana, who's sitting right next to him. I wonder what the story is there. "And I don't have to continue looking for a new condo for you, Zeke?"

Cherry's face whips around to mine. "You were looking for a *new* condo?"

"Let's talk about this later."

"Oh, we're going to talk about it, all right. I can't *believe* you."

"Oops," Indigo says with a cringe. "Sorry."

"Smooth move," Montana mutters, rolling her eyes.

"What in the hell am I missing over there?" I demand, but Indigo doesn't reply, and Montana just shakes her head.

"Drama," Wolfe whispers.

"I heard that," Montana says.

"I wasn't trying that hard to cover it up," Wolfe replies with a grin. "Good to know your ears work."

"You're funny," Montana replies, but from the look on her face, it's safe to say that she doesn't find Wolfe funny at all.

"Hey, I have fun news," Luna announces, changing the subject. "I know the inn isn't officially open yet, but I want to have a girls' night out there. I think it's going to become a regular, monthly thing, and I need to try it out. All of you are invited. And the ladies from Three Sisters Kitchen will cater. I need to make sure it's something fun that I can pull off regularly."

"Honey, you know we're in," Sarah says. "When? And what can we bring?"

"I know it's short notice, but I'd love to do it tomorrow night."

"My girl is nothing if not spontaneous," Wolfe says with a grin.

"I told you, it's short notice," Luna says, wincing. "But I'm losing time between now and when we officially open, and I really want to try this out."

"I'm in," Cherry says. "Montana?"

"Of course. Need ice cream?"

"Hey, maybe. I think it would be fun to feature different things from women-owned businesses each month."

"I think that's a great idea," Montana says, getting excited. "Did you know that Cherry makes candles and room sprays and all kinds of cool things?"

I feel Cherry fidget next to me as Luna shifts her attention. "How did I not know this? Do you mean to tell me that I could feature locally sourced candles and other fancy goodies in our guest rooms? This is huge! I need to place a giant order, Cherry. Where is your storefront? It must be new."

"Oh, I don't have one. Don't tell my HOA, but I do my work online and out of my guest room."

I sit back smugly and listen to Sarah, Luna, and Montana try to talk some sense into Cherry about starting a business. I couldn't agree with them more, and I wish Cherry would listen to them.

"Girl, I've been telling you this for more than two years. You could make *bank*. There is a huge demand for what you offer."

"Too risky," Cherry says, shaking her head. "But thanks for the vote of confidence. I'd love to talk to you about putting my products in the inn, Luna."

"Oh, you can bet your fine ass we'll be talking," Luna promises just as someone turns on the microphone to get the rest of the night underway.

* * * *

"Okay, that was *fun*," Cherry announces as we step inside my condo, and she kicks out of her heels, sighing in relief. "Those things were killing me. Montana's feet are just a tiny bit smaller than mine."

"Wait." I hold up a hand and scowl. "You were wearing Montana's shoes?"

"Well, sure. I don't have heels to go with that dress. It would be silly to buy new ones for just one night."

"No, silly is walking in shoes that don't fucking fit you, Cherry."

She narrows her eyes at me and, without a word, walks right into the guest room and shuts the door.

Five minutes later, she walks back out, sans dress and wearing some leggings with a loose top, her hair up in a ponytail.

"If you want to argue," she begins, "let's talk about something more important than shoes. You never told me that you were looking for a new place to live."

"Of course, I didn't. Why would I tell you that? You were the reason I wanted to move. But things have changed. Besides, there are no other beachfront condos in this town."

Cherry's eyes narrow further. "Why was I the reason you wanted to move, Zeke?"

"Come on." I blow out a breath and push my hand through my hair. "You know why. We didn't get along *at all*. We made each other's lives a living hell, and it was getting to where I didn't want to even be at home anymore."

"Well—"

"No, pull the stick out of your ass, Cherry. I'm not done. The past few weeks have been awesome, and I know without a doubt that this is where I want to be. With you. I don't need to move, and now that we've ironed things out, there's no reason to. Come on, you have to admit that before Halloween, we didn't enjoy living across from each other."

She looks like she wants to argue, but then she deflates. "Okay, I admit it. But you should have said something."

"I'll be honest, the minute you knocked on my door, all wet and naked and adorable, I completely forgot about moving. There was nothing to tell you because it wasn't going to happen."

Her expression softens, and I know I'm off the hook.

"That was a good answer."

"Move in with me."

The words are out before I've even fully formed them in my head, but I don't regret voicing them.

"Huh?"

"Move in here." I walk over to her and take her hand in mine, linking our fingers. "You've been practically living here anyway, and I like it. Besides, you said before that you've always had your eye on this unit."

"I'm not moving in with you for the view."

"Okay, move in with me for the sex."

She snorts, and I lean down to kiss her.

"Then you can sell your condo and pursue your new business."

I lean in for another kiss, but she plants her hand on my chest, stopping me.

"What?"

Chapter Seven

Cherry

"*What* did you just say?" I demand, backing away from him.

"That once you sell your condo to move in here, you'll be able to use the equity to start your business."

"I don't know how many times I have to say this tonight, but I'm fine with how things are. If I sell my condo, it's because I'll have bills to pay *here* when I move in with you. And right now, that's a big *if.*"

He presses his fingers into his eyes and sighs loudly. "Do whatever you want, Cherry. Work at the school, make candles, or start walking tours through town, I don't fucking *care*. I just want you to be happy and do what fulfills you. But you won't be paying any bills here, I can tell you that right now."

I blink at him for five full seconds. "Are you a caveman?"

"No, I've already got the bills covered. I don't need you to pay them."

"I don't need a sugar daddy."

"Oh, for fuck's sake." He begins to pace, clearly frustrated. "Wanting to have you with me all the time is a crime? Wanting to take care of you?"

"I don't need—"

"You've made it abundantly clear to me that you don't *need* me, any more than I need you to function as a productive member of society. That's not what this is about. I want to do those things because I care about you. Damn it, I've managed to fall in love with you over the past few weeks, and I want the partnership."

"No." I shake my head, my frustration waging a war inside of me. "You want to decide how I live my life, with a new business and not paying any of my own bills."

"You've got to be kidding me," he mutters, hanging his head. "If that's what you think about me, you don't know me at all, Cherry. And we're just wasting our time here."

My heart is pounding. I *know* that I'm saying all the wrong things, totally sabotaging this, but I don't know how to accept love and help, and I don't know how to fix it.

"I just mean—"

"I get it," is all he says, interrupting me. "Look, maybe we need to take a night off, you know? Simmer down a bit."

My mouth drops open, then closes again. "You're kicking me out?"

"Let's just take the night." He moves to walk past me toward his bedroom. He doesn't touch me as he passes. He doesn't even look at me.

And I know, without a shadow of a doubt, that I've just fucked it all up.

* * * *

"You look like hell," Montana says when she picks me up to go to girls' night out at the inn. "What happened?"

"I didn't sleep," I reply and buckle my seat belt. I tried to get out of going tonight, but Montana wouldn't hear of it and insisted that we ride together. "I should drive myself because I don't know how long I'll stay."

"That's perfect because I can't stay late either. I have an early dentist appointment tomorrow. Did you bring your candle samples?"

"Shit." I unbuckle the belt. "Be right back."

"Need help?"

"Nah, it's fine."

"Cheer up. We're going to have *fun*."

But I don't reply as I walk back up the stairs to my condo, key my way inside, and grab the small box of goodies that I brought for Luna to try out. If she buys stock to put in all of her guest rooms, that would be a huge sale for me.

On my way back out, I run smack dab into Zeke, and my heart gives a little lurch in my chest.

"Hi," I say softly.

He looks like he doesn't want to reply, as if he thought he'd already missed me, but he nods.

"Hey. Let me get that."

Before I can object, he takes the box from me.

"Montana and I are going to that girls' night out thing at the inn."

"Should be fun." I hate how short he is, how distant, and I wish with all my might that I knew how to fix this.

When we reach Montana's car, he sets the box in the back seat and makes a move to leave.

"Zeke."

He stops and turns to me, one eyebrow raised in question, but I don't know what to say.

"Can we talk later?"

He licks his lips and looks away, but then he nods. Hope fills me. "Text me when you're home."

"I will. Thanks."

I get back into Montana's car, and she watches Zeke walk away.

"Whoa, what the hell happened since the gala last night?"

"I don't want to talk about it."

"Honey, I'm sorry if things aren't working out."

"I don't know what things are right now," I admit and stare out the passenger window as Montana drives through Huckleberry Bay toward the inn at the top of the cliffs, right next to the lighthouse. I've always loved it up here, and longed to see the inside of the lighthouse, to walk along the cliffs.

But it's never been open to the public, at least until Luna decided to build the inn, Luna's Light. It opens just before Christmas next month, with a huge holiday party for everyone in town. I can't wait for it. I'm even going to buy a new dress for the occasion, and probably even splurge on getting my hair done.

"It's so pretty up here," Montana says as we climb the road that leads to the lighthouse. "So green, even in the fall."

I nod in agreement, and then the lighthouse comes into view, along with the new inn just a short distance away.

We park and walk to the portico where the entrance to the inn is. The door is open, and we can hear people already talking and laughing inside.

There's a huge foyer with a grand staircase that leads upstairs, but we walk straight down a hallway to a dining area where everyone is gathered.

There are even accordion-style doors that open on a pass-through to the kitchen, so dishes can be easily transferred to the dining room without having to walk around.

"This is *incredible*," I breathe, and Luna turns with a big smile.

"You're here! I'm so happy to have you guys. As you can see, we have drinks and lots of food. You know Mira, the chef at Three Sisters. Well, she's the chef here, too, and she's outdone herself on the menu, so have one of everything."

"Luna, this is amazing," Montana says with a little bounce. "The inn is just gorgeous."

"Thank you." Luna beams at the compliment. "I can't wait for the rest of the town to see it in just a few weeks. I can't believe we're almost there."

"Everyone is so proud of you," Montana says and wraps her arms around Luna in a hug. "So damn proud."

"Don't go making me cry." Luna wipes a tear from her eye and turns her attention to me. "Did you bring fun stuff for me?"

"Of course, I did. These aren't all the scents I offer, but there's a nice selection to try. And if you want something else, we can work up something unique and exclusive to the inn."

"Oh, I *love* that idea," Luna exclaims but then looks at me closer. "Are you okay, Cherry?"

I probably shouldn't have come tonight. I *hate* being the center of attention.

"I'm fine."

"You don't look fine," Sarah adds as she joins us. Their third best friend, June, comes over as well and frowns at me.

"Have you been crying?" June asks. "Liquor. That'll help."

"It's just been a shitty day," I begin, but I'm pulled to a table where someone sets a drink and a heaping plate of food in front of me. Suddenly, I'm surrounded by Luna, Sarah, June, Montana, and even Amaryllis Lovejoy, Indigo's sister.

"Tell us everything," Luna invites. "This is girls' night out. This is what we're here for."

"It is?" I ask with uncertainty.

"We're not here to knit, honey," Amaryllis says. "We're here to vent, laugh, cry, solve the world's problems. You're up first. What's up?"

For a moment, all I can do is stare at the women watching me with curiosity, and then I smile. "Zeke is an asshole."

Okay, so maybe not an *asshole*, but I just don't know what to do with him, and I need to talk about him behind his back to sympathetic friends. Plus, he told me he loved me, and I said *nothing*. Because I panicked.

"Man trouble," June says with a nod. "We're here for it. What did he do?"

"He says he wants me to move in with him. That I can sell my condo and start my business."

They're quiet for a moment, and then all frown.

"And then what did he do to piss you off?" Montana asks.

"That. That's what he did. And he said that I don't have to pay any bills at his condo."

"Hold up." Amaryllis shakes her head. "That pissed you off?"

"Yes! I'm not a kept woman. I don't need to be taken care of. And I keep telling him that I don't want to start my own business because it's too risky. I need the stability of a regular paycheck. It's like he just doesn't listen to me. He said he wants to *take care of me*, like I'm a puppy or something. I've been taking care of myself since I was a kid."

I'm all riled up again, and I reach for the glass of champagne, taking a long drink.

"First of all," Luna says, after sticking her nose in one of my candles, "these are *amazing*. The labeling is adorable, and I can tell the quality is fabulous."

"They're all-natural," I reply, my voice still hard from being frustrated.

I glance at Montana and see she's just sitting there, her arms folded, a smug smile on her pretty face as she watches me.

"What?"

"I've already voiced my opinion on this ad nauseum. I'm going to let them tell you for a change."

"Tell me what?"

"That you need to start a business," June says, shoving a canapé in her mouth. "I mean, if you hate Zeke, fine, fuck him, but the business thing should happen. Because you're smart, make nice things, and people will buy them. You live in a tourist town. If you don't want to open a shop, which I totally get, you could put your stuff on consignment in the bookstore, at the inn, the coffee shop, and other places. I'm telling you, people love that smelly stuff."

"Told you," Montana says.

"I'll happily make room for a cabinet for you to display your goods for sale," Luna offers with a new, excited glint in her eye. "I'll offer the candles, sprays, and bath bombs for use in the rooms, and guests will love them so much, they'll buy them in the lobby."

"Absolutely," Amaryllis agrees, also smelling one of the candles. "Hell, can I buy this right now?"

"Next month," Luna decides. "For girls' night out next month, you'll be my first featured women's business."

"Oh, I don't know."

"You should listen to me more," Montana says. "I wouldn't steer you wrong. I *love* you. I want you to kick ass."

"You're my best friend," I tell her. "You're *supposed* to hype me up. That doesn't mean the business will take off."

"Maybe you need to have as much confidence in yourself as Montana and Zeke have in you," Sarah says thoughtfully, tapping her finger on her chin.

"Are you guys telling me that Zeke wasn't the asshole last night?"

"I really hate it when the man isn't the asshole," June grumbles. "But, yeah. Sounds like he cares about you."

"He used the *L*-word."

Montana giggles. The others smile.

"And what did you say?" Luna asks.

"I told him that he wants to control me."

"Yikes," Amaryllis says, and the others lose their smiles. I feel awful all over again. "I don't think he sounded controlling. He wants you to succeed, and maybe taking care of the household bills while you pursue your passion is his way of helping you do that."

"I'm not good at the love stuff," I admit. "But, yeah, that was a dick move on my part. And then he kicked me out of his condo and told me that we needed to take the night off."

"You hurt his feelings," Sarah says softly. "That's what it sounds like to me."

"*That's* what I'm good at. Arguing and being irritated by him. Jabbing at him. It's a habit I've had since he moved into the place. How am I supposed to change overnight?"

"Do you love him back?" Luna asks.

I blink at her and feel my stomach tie itself into knots. Do I *love* Zeke? He's helpful and hard working. He's funny. The sex is ridiculously out of this world. And he can be really tender at times, which is something that I didn't know I needed but absolutely do.

Shit. I'm totally in love with Zeke.

"Yeah." I swallow hard. "I do, and it makes me sad that I hurt his feelings."

"You need to tell *him* that," Amaryllis says. "You need to be open with him. And vulnerable."

"Yikes."

Amaryllis laughs. "I know, it's hard. But it doesn't sound like he wants to control you. He wants a partnership. That's what happens in a partnership. You're vulnerable, and you take care of each other. You can pay some of the bills, but it sounds like he wants to take that burden off your shoulders so you *can* start the business you want with a safety net under you. Because he probably knows that you need the stability."

I think back to our picnic on the beach and the conversation we had.

He really is trying to help.

"Luna, this was a ton of fun, and I'll be here every month with bells on, but I think I'd better go home and eat some crow now."

Montana, laughing hysterically, stands and grabs her bag. "Let's go. I'm totally coming back for more food, but I'm her ride, so I'm going to get her home."

"Hurry," I say when we're in the car and Montana is headed down the hill. "I need to fix this before he decides to break up with me for good."

"He won't decide that. I saw the way he looked at you last night. You just have to find a way to not be so defensive all the time, Cherry. Not everyone is your parents."

"I know. I *know* that, but it's not easy."

"You can do it. I have faith in you."

Chapter Eight

Zeke

I think I have everything ready.

Except myself.

Because I'm nervous as fuck.

Cherry pissed me off so badly last night that I almost called off the entire relationship. While up all night, going over everything in my head, I wondered if the constant bantering and hurt feelings are worth it with her.

But then I also remembered all the good times we've had lately, which far outweigh the bad, and I started to miss her like crazy.

When I saw her in the hall earlier, it was a punch to the solar plexus. And I knew without a doubt that I'd do anything in my power to have her because no one in my entire life has ever made me feel as alive as Cherry has.

Suddenly, there's a knock on my door, and I frown. I'm not expecting anyone, and Cherry should be at the girls' night thing for a while yet.

But when I answer it, there she is, wide-eyed and looking as nervous as I feel.

"You're back."

"Yeah." She swallows hard and wrings her hands. "Can I please come in?"

"Sure." I step back, and she walks across the threshold, then gasps.

"What's this?"

"Well, you're early, so the surprise isn't all finished yet, but it's for you."

I follow her gaze, taking in the unlit candles, the flowers, and the table set for dessert. Because she's here early, there's even a killer sunset happening on the water below.

Without a word, she turns and throws herself into my arms, holding on tightly enough to stay on a bucking bronco.

"I'm so sorry," she says, her voice full of tears. "I'm *so* sorry. You didn't deserve what I said last night at all, and I was a complete jerk because I got nervous and probably a little irritated, but mostly nervous."

"Whoa, baby." Wrapping my arms around her, I kiss the top of her head. "We'll talk in a second. First, this feels good."

"Yeah." But she can't stay still long before she pulls back and looks up at me. "Okay, we need to talk now because it's making me crazy."

"Let's sit. Do you want something to drink?"

"Water. Water would be good."

"You got it."

Cherry perches on my couch, and I walk into the kitchen to grab a couple of waters, then join her, taking the seat across from her.

Because if I sit next to her, I'll just snuggle her, and we have some things to clear up first.

"Thanks." She sips, then sets the bottle aside. "I feel really awful. I don't want to fight with you anymore. I think that a year of that is enough."

"Agreed. But we always seem to dissolve into an argument or a misunderstanding of some kind, and I don't want that either."

"I get defensive," she admits softly. "And that's stupid because you've done nothing but show me that you have my back and that you understand me."

"Old habits die hard."

"Yeah, well, they need to die completely, because if they don't, this relationship won't work. Words matter, Zeke, and I said some really hurtful things to you last night."

"Yes, you did."

Her eyes fill with tears again.

"I'm so sorry. You were being so sweet, and I *would* love to live here with you. I mean, sure, we're moving pretty fast, but we're adults, and the bottom line is...I love you, too."

My heart stops, and I hold my breath. This is exactly what I'd needed to hear last night.

"I think you and everyone else are right about the business," she continues as if she didn't just make everything in the world right again. "It scares me, but I think I can make a good living from what I create, and I'd like the chance to try. But, Zeke, I wasn't lying last night when I said I'm not a kept woman. I *want* to help financially because that's what a partnership is."

"Okay."

She blinks at me. "Okay?"

"Sure. You want to pay the utilities? That's fine with me. Groceries? Great. But what I was trying to say last night is that I want you to have the opportunity to pursue your passion without worrying about bills, even if it's just once in your life. I understand needing stability. But, sweetheart, that's *me*. I'm your stability."

"You're too far away."

Cherry hurries over to me and climbs into my lap, wrapping her arms around my neck.

"I was so worried that I'd fucked it all up for good," she whispers, burying her face in my neck. "And I had to come here to grovel."

"I was going to apologize tonight," I admit. "Give you flowers and tiramisu and figure out a way to make it all work."

"You have tiramisu?" Her head comes up, and she smiles. "You *are* trying hard. But you don't need to apologize."

"Yeah, I do. Because I didn't explain myself well, I just started talking, saying what I want, but I didn't give you time to come around to it. We didn't have an adult conversation about it."

"We need to work on that since we don't hate each other anymore."

"You're right." I kiss her forehead, so relieved that the Earth has shifted back on its axis. "How do you feel about us waiting on the dessert?"

"What do you have in mind?"

I drag my fingers down her cheek, her neck, and outline her collarbone. "I want to be inside you."

"Dessert can wait for that."

Before I can lift her, she hops off my lap and practically skips to the bedroom.

When I make it to the threshold of my room, she's already half-naked.

"I was going to do that." But I lean on the doorjamb, cross my arms over my chest, and enjoy the show.

"You're slow," she replies. "You were way back there, so I decided to get this party started."

I laugh and push away from the door, stalking toward her, relieved that she's here and will be staying.

And later, when we're both panting and pleasantly exhausted, an idea occurs to me.

"You know, if you plan to sell the condo, you'll *have* to get the hot water heater fixed."

Cherry snorts with laughter. "I guess so. I'll call around tomorrow."

"I'm going to miss that heater."

She lifts her head and frowns up at me. "Why?"

"Because without that piece of crap, you wouldn't be here. With me."

"Oh, I don't know. I think we would have gotten around to it eventually."

Epilogue

It's been nice to be able to slowly move my things over to Zeke's condo.

Well, *our* condo now.

It took a full week to decide how we were going to integrate all our stuff. We didn't have room for two couches, two dining sets, and well, two of just about everything.

But with very little arguing, we figured it out and kept the castoffs in my old condo so we could take everything over to Samson House for donations when the time came, and someone else could get life out of the things that Zeke and I didn't need.

"I think that's it," Zeke says as he sets the last box in the moving truck we rented for the occasion. We have some fragile things in the back of my SUV, and I reach up to hit the button to close it. Zeke fixed that for me last week, and I have to admit, the gesture made me swoon. He seems to find ways to do that to me often these days. "Let's head out."

"I'll follow you."

"No, we'll come back for the stuff in the car later. I want to go together."

I shrug and climb up into the truck.

"I'm so excited." I buckle my seat belt in the truck that sits super high up, my stomach jittering. "So many people can use these things."

"There's some good stuff in there," he agrees. "I still say we should have kept my dining room set."

"It looked like something out of a gothic horror novel," I reply, rolling my eyes. "Where did you even get it?"

"It was on clearance in Alabama years ago."

"Exactly. It was on *clearance* because no one else wanted that monstrosity. But I think someone could sand it down, paint it something other than black, and make it nice. I just don't have the time for it."

"Not to mention, you hate it."

I grin over at him. "I really do. Sorry, babe."

"It's just a dining set." He shrugs and pulls into the Samson House parking lot, where they accept donations.

When I jump out of the truck, I'm surprised to find that we're not the only ones here.

In fact, there must be a dozen trucks of all shapes and sizes, and our friends are stepping out of them.

Luna and Wolfe, Sarah and Tanner, June and her new husband, Apollo. Montana, Indigo, Amaryllis, and so many others from town are all grinning big as they hurry over to us.

"What are you guys doing?"

"We decided to make this a *huge* donation day," Montana says with a proud grin, winking at Zeke.

"What did you do?" I ask him.

"This is my town now," he says with a shrug. "I know people. And we decided that we'd all support you today."

I don't know if I've ever loved anyone more as I lean in and kiss Zeke's shoulder.

"Thank you," I whisper and then turn back to the others. "Thank you all so much."

"No, thank *you*," June says with a laugh. "Thanks to you, I managed to purge a hell of a lot of stuff out of Annabelle's house. That woman never throws anything away."

"There's no need to throw it away," the manager of Samson House says as she walks outside. "Because we'll happily take it. Let's get started, shall we?"

Everyone returns to their trucks to dig in and get everything organized, but I turn to Zeke first.

"I love you so much for this."

"Just for this?"

"It tops the list right now, yes. Thank you."

"If you're happy, I'm happy, baby."

We ended up at Lighthouse Pizza for some lunchtime food, pool, karaoke, and darts with all our friends.

And now that we're back home, I'm sitting on the balcony, taking in the sunset over the ocean. The clouds are moody, but they broke long enough to give us an amazing show.

Zeke opens the sliding door and joins me, passing me some wine.

"I'll never get tired of this view." I clink my glass to his in cheers and then take a sip.

"Me, neither," Zeke says, but when I turn to look at him, I find him watching me.

"You're smitten."

"Oh, absolutely."

"I love the painting Sarah did for above the couch." I crane my neck so I can look in the window at the big seascape that now hangs in our living room. "She's just so dang *good.*"

"She put the dog in the painting," Zeke says casually.

"And it's adorable."

"I was thinking, what if we got a real dog to go with the painting?"

I blink over at him. "Really?"

"Don't you like dogs?"

"Of course, I like dogs. What's not to like? But we're kind of busy right now finalizing the sale of the other condo, getting my store going, and everything else."

"I can take the dog to the garage with me. And I'm sure you could take it with you to your shop once it's open."

My heart stutters at that. I managed to sell my condo for much more than the asking price, thanks to Indigo Lovejoy. And I'll have plenty of money to buy a little storefront in downtown Huckleberry Bay, where I can make all my products and even hold classes to teach others how to do it, as well.

I'm so damn excited, I can hardly contain myself.

"Baby?"

"Yeah, I could probably do that. But puppies are so much work, Zeke."

"Maybe not a puppy." He sips his wine. "Maybe we visit the shelter and rescue someone who needs a home."

"How many times are you going to make me cry today?" I wipe at a tear and then laugh when he just smiles at me. "Yes, I think that's a good idea."

"Good deal." He reaches over for my hand. "Our family is already growing."

Our family.

That might be the best thing I've ever heard.

* * * *

Also from 1001 Dark Nights and Kristen Proby, discover The Scramble, Change With Me, Shine With Me, Wonder With Me, Soaring With Fallon, Tempting Brooke, No Reservations, Easy With You, Easy For Keeps, and Indulge With Me.

Sign up for the 1001 Dark Nights Newsletter
and be entered to win a Tiffany Key necklace.

There's a contest every month!

Go to www.1001DarkNights.com to subscribe.

**As a bonus, all subscribers can download
FIVE FREE exclusive books!**

Discover 1001 Dark Nights Collection Ten

DRAGON LOVER by Donna Grant
A Dragon Kings Novella

KEEPING YOU by Aurora Rose Reynolds
An Until Him/Her Novella

HAPPILY EVER NEVER by Carrie Ann Ryan
A Montgomery Ink Legacy Novella

DESTINED FOR ME by Corinne Michaels
A Come Back for Me/Say You'll Stay Crossover

MADAM ALANA by Audrey Carlan
A Marriage Auction Novella

DIRTY FILTHY BILLIONAIRE by Laurelin Paige
A Dirty Universe Novella

HIDE AND SEEK by Laura Kaye
A Blasphemy Novella

TANGLED WITH YOU by J. Kenner
A Stark Security Novella

TEMPTED by Lexi Blake
A Masters and Mercenaries Novella

THE DANDELION DIARY by Devney Perry
A Maysen Jar Novella

CHERRY LANE by Kristen Proby
A Huckleberry Bay Novella

THE GRAVE ROBBER by Darynda Jones
A Charley Davidson Novella

CRY OF THE BANSHEE by Heather Graham
A Krewe of Hunters Novella

DARKEST NEED by Rachel Van Dyken
A Dark Ones Novella

CHRISTMAS IN CAPE MAY by Jennifer Probst
A Sunshine Sisters Novella

A VAMPIRE'S MATE by Rebecca Zanetti
A Dark Protectors/Rebels Novella

WHERE IT BEGINS by Helena Hunting
A Pucked Novella

Also from Blue Box Press

THE MARRIAGE AUCTION by Audrey Carlan
Season One, Volume One
Season One, Volume Two
Season One, Volume Three
Season One, Volume Four

THE JEWELER OF STOLEN DREAMS by M.J. Rose

SAPPHIRE STORM by Christopher Rice writing as C. Travis Rice
A Sapphire Cove Novel

ATLAS: THE STORY OF PA SALT by Lucinda Riley and Harry
Whittaker

LOVE ON THE BYLINE by Xio Axelrod
A Plays and Players Novel

A SOUL OF ASH AND BLOOD by Jennifer L. Armentrout
A Blood and Ash Novel

START US UP by Lexi Blake
A Park Avenue Promise Novel

FIGHTING THE PULL by Kristen Ashley
A River Rain Novel

A FIRE IN THE FLESH by Jennifer L. Armentrout
A Flesh and Fire Novel

Discover More Kristen Proby

The Scramble: A Single in Seattle Novella

There are two things you need to know about me. 1: I'm never late. And 2: I hate Christmas. Yes, I'm a girl who hates the holidays.

My entire, enormous family is already enjoying their holiday vacation in Iceland, but thanks to my busy job and having to meet them there, I'm late. They could have chosen *any* holiday to fly across the world, but Christmas won, which sent me scrambling because the end of the year is my busiest time. It's difficult to carve out moments to see the family at all.

So, now, I'm forty thousand feet in the air, trying to get to Iceland before Christmas morning, all while also attempting to get some work done. If only the hot guy next to me would leave me be.

Dylan says I should put the work away until after my holiday and relax a bit. And while his suggestion of spending some time together on the north Atlantic island seems preposterous, I can't help but feel intrigued when he promises to show me how to enjoy the Yuletide season properly.

After all, I can't possibly spend *every* minute with my family.

But how do I just shrug off my duty to my job and throw caution to the wind for a stranger...no matter how handsome he is? Because that's something else about me: I never throw caution to the wind—even a beautiful, blustery Icelandic wind.

Then again, Mama always said, *"Never say never..."*

* * * *

Change With Me: A With Me In Seattle Novella

Zane Cooper. Hollywood royalty. Fourth generation superstar. He knows what it is to be one of the biggest celebrities in the world. And how lonely that title truly is. When scandal hits, his career hangs in the balance, and Zane flees LA for Seattle, laying low with his newly married best friend. Things will eventually blow over, and he'll have his life back soon enough.

Aubrey Stansfield arrives in Seattle excited to start a new job, and eager to settle into her new home. But when she arrives at her rental, Aubrey's sure she's imagining things because the uber sexy Zane Cooper is unpacking in *her* new bedroom. Thanks to a rental snafu, and unwilling to relocate on such short notice, Aubrey and Zane are thrust into being roommates.

Aubrey is about as average as a woman gets, so what could the megastar possibly see in her? She tells herself she's not interested, despite their undeniable chemistry. But Zane is very persuasive, and soon Aubrey finds herself playing house with the most recognized man on the planet. Deep down, she knows it's all a fantasy. He'll head back to his posh lifestyle soon and leave her behind. No way could she fall in love with him.

But love doesn't always follow the rules…

* * * *

Shine With Me: A With Me In Seattle Novella

Sabrina Harrison *hates* being famous. She walked away from show business, from the flashing bulbs and prying eyes years ago, and is happy in her rural Oregon home, dedicating her life to her non-profit.

Until Hollywood calls, offering her the role of a lifetime. In more than ten years, she's never felt the pull to return to the business that shunned her, but this role is everything Sabrina's ever longed for.

Now she has to get in shape for it.

Benjamin Demarco's gym, Sound Fitness, continues making a name for itself in Seattle. And now, he finds himself with the task of training Sabrina, getting her in shape for the role of her life. He's trained hundreds of women. This is his job. So why does he suddenly see Sabrina as more than just another client? His hands linger on her skin, his breath catches when she's near.

He knows better. Soon, she'll be gone, living her life. A life that doesn't include him.

* * * *

Wonder With Me: With Me In Seattle Novella

Reed Taylor doesn't pay much attention to the holidays—until he receives a surprise present. Four-year-old Piper is the daughter he never knew about, and with the death of her mother, is also now the roommate he never expected. He's determined to make their first Christmas together one she'll never forget.

Noel Thompson has gotten her share of strange requests in her career as an interior designer. The call to design a beautiful home for Christmas is more like a dream come true. And that was *before* she met her new employer—sexy and mysterious, he's everything she ever hoped Santa would bring her.

As Noel showers his home with holiday spirit, Reed showers Piper with love. And the busy life he's created for himself no longer seems nearly as important as the one Noel is helping him build with his daughter. But if he can't convince his decorator to stay, this could be the only year he feels the true wonder of the season.

* * * *

Tempting Brooke: A Big Sky Novella

Brooke's Blooms has taken Cunningham Falls by surprise. The beautiful, innovative flower shop is trendy, with not only gorgeous flower arrangements, but also fun gifts for any occasion. This store is Brooke Henderson's deepest joy, and it means everything to her, which shows in how completely she and her little shop have been embraced by the small community of Cunningham Falls.

So, when her landlord dies and Brody Chabot saunters through her door, announcing that the building has been sold, and will soon be demolished, Brooke knows that she's in for the fight of her life. But she hasn't gotten this far by sitting back and quietly doing what she's told. *Hustle* is Brooke's middle name, and she has no intention of losing this fight, no matter how tempting Brody's smile -- and body -- is.

* * * *

No Reservations: A Fusion Novella

Chase MacKenzie is *not* the man for Maura Jenkins. A self-proclaimed life-long bachelor, and unapologetic about his distaste for monogamy, a woman would have to be a masochist to want to fall into Chase's bed.

And Maura is no masochist.

Chase has one strict rule: no strings attached. Which is fine with Maura because she doesn't even really *like* Chase. He's arrogant, cocky, and let's not forget bossy. But when he aims that crooked grin at her, she goes weak in the knees. Not that she has any intentions of falling for his charms.

Definitely not.

Well, maybe just once…

* * * *

Easy For Keeps: A Boudreaux Novella

Adam Spencer loves women. All women. Every shape and size, regardless of hair or eye color, religion or race, he simply enjoys them all. Meeting more than his fair share as the manager and head bartender of The Odyssey, a hot spot in the heart of New Orleans' French Quarter, Adam's comfortable with his lifestyle, and sees no reason to change it. A wife and kids, plus the white picket fence are not in the cards for this confirmed bachelor. Until a beautiful woman, and her sweet princess, literally knock him on his ass.

Sarah Cox has just moved to New Orleans, having accepted a position as a social worker specializing in at-risk women and children. It's a demanding, sometimes dangerous job, but Sarah is no shy wallflower. She can handle just about anything that comes at her, even the attentions of one sexy Adam Spencer. Just because he's charmed her daughter, making her think of magical kingdoms with happily ever after, doesn't mean that Sarah believes in fairy tales. But the more time she spends with the enchanting man, the more he begins to sway her into believing in forever.

Even so, when Sarah's job becomes more dangerous than any of them bargained for, will she be ripped from Adam's life forever?

* * * *

Easy With You: A With You In Seattle Novella

Nothing has ever come easy for Lila Bailey. She's fought for every good thing in her life during every day of her thirty-one years. Aside from that one night with an impossible to deny stranger a year ago, Lila is the epitome of responsible.

Steadfast. Strong.

She's pulled herself out of the train wreck of her childhood, proud to be a professor at Tulane University and laying down roots in a city she's grown to love. But when some of her female students are viciously murdered, Lila's shaken to the core and unsure of whom she can trust in New Orleans. When the police detective assigned to the murder case comes to investigate, she's even more surprised to find herself staring into the eyes of the man that made her toes curl last year.

In an attempt to move on from the tragic loss of his wife, Asher Smith moved his daughter and himself to a new city, ready for a fresh start. A damn fine police lieutenant, but new to the New Orleans force, Asher has a lot to prove to his colleagues and himself.

With a murderer terrorizing the Tulane University campus, Asher finds himself toe-to-toe with the one woman that haunts his dreams. His hands, his lips, his body know her as intimately as he's ever known anyone. As he learns her mind and heart as well, Asher wants nothing more than to keep her safe, in his bed, and in his and his daughter's lives for the long haul.

But when Lila becomes the target, can Asher save her in time, or will he lose another woman he loves?

* * * *

Soaring with Fallon: A Big Sky Novel

Fallon McCarthy has climbed the corporate ladder. She's had the office with the view, the staff, and the plaque on her door. The unexpected loss of her grandmother taught her that there's more to life than meetings and conference calls, so she quit, and is happy to be a nomad, checking off items on her bucket list as she takes jobs teaching yoga in each place she lands in. She's happy being free, and has no interest in being tied down.

When Noah King gets the call that an eagle has been injured, he's not expecting to find a beautiful stranger standing vigil when he arrives. Rehabilitating birds of prey is Noah's passion, it's what he lives for, and he doesn't have time for a nosy woman who's suddenly taken an interest in Spread Your Wings sanctuary.

But Fallon's gentle nature, and the way she makes him laugh, and *feel* again draws him in. When it comes time for Fallon to move on, will Noah's love be enough for her to stay, or will he have to find the strength to let her fly?

* * * *

Indulge With Me: A With Me In Seattle Celebration
Short stories by Kristen Proby
Recipes from Suzanne M. Johnson

The beloved Montgomery Family, from New York Times Bestselling author Kristen Proby's With Me In Seattle series, is big, and it just keeps growing! There are parties and celebrations taking place at every turn, and we are delighted to invite you to all of the festivities!

Whether it's a brunch hosted by Nate and Jules McKenna, or a fancy dinner party hosted by Luke and Natalie Williams, you won't want to miss all we have in store for you! Each all-new story will feature shenanigans, laughter, love and lots of food.

And let's not forget cocktails!

Kristen, along with USA Today Bestselling author Suzanne Johnson, have teamed up to bring you this cookbook, celebrating family, love, and absolutely delicious foods, perfect for any occasion.

So sit back, or march straight into the kitchen, and get ready to indulge. We hope you're hungry!

Lighthouse Way
A Huckleberry Bay Novel
By Kristen Proby
Now available!

From *NYT* best-selling Author Kristen Proby comes an all new epic series about three best friends, a local legend, and finding love on the stunning Oregon Coast!

Luna Winchester's life is firmly entrenched in the coastal town Huckleberry Bay, Oregon. A fourth-generation light keeper, Luna is carrying on the Winchester tradition by tending to the lighthouse. Plus, she's decided to renovate a long-abandoned building on the property and make it a B&B, Luna's Light. Surrounded by family and her two childhood best friends, her life is full.

Wolfe Conrad is in hiding, and he's come to Huckleberry Bay to heal. A career-ending accident on the track nearly took his life, and now he seeks refuge to try and build a new one. The quaint town's slow pace rattles the man who's first love is fast cars—and then there's the beautiful innkeeper, who rattles him in different ways.

Falling in love with Luna definitely isn't part of Wolfe's plan. Local legends that tell of unrequited love and despair? Unbelievable. But stranger things have happened, like two strangers falling in love...

* * * *

Chapter One
~Wolfe~

"It's my distinct pleasure to introduce a man who needs no introduction at all," Mayor Rebecca Schlinger says with a wide grin as she looks over at me. "Our own hometown pride and joy, Wolfe Conrad!"

It seems that all two thousand and nine citizens of Huckleberry Bay are in the crowd, cheering and waving their arms and flags as I take the stage and smile out at them.

It's the Fourth of July Festival in my hometown of Huckleberry Bay, and I'm here as a celebrity guest—and to drive in the dirt races for charity.

I'm used to loud crowds and exuberant fans, but this hits a little differently. Okay, a *lot* differently.

Because this is home, and the crowd cheering right now is full of friends and people I've known for most of my life. I lit out of here as fast as I could after high school, obsessed with cars and driving fast. Hell, I haven't even been back home since my parents died almost two years ago, within months of each other. My dad died from cancer, and my mom passed from what I'm sure was a broken heart.

Yet, still, the people here are proud of me.

And there's nothing like the Oregon coast in the summertime.

"Thank you," I call out into the microphone, and the crowd starts to quiet so they can hear me. "It's always good to be home, and I'm glad I could be here for this. You know, when I was a kid, this festival was my favorite time of year. We're going to put on an exciting race for you all today and raise some money for the local food bank while we're at it."

I let my gaze skim over the familiar faces, pausing when I see Luna Winchester. I lift a brow at her, and she smiles.

It's been a lot longer than two years since I saw Luna.

I send her a wink and then get back to the task at hand.

Racing. My lifeblood. It's always a thrill to drive, but doing it in my hometown? Well, there's an added layer of adrenaline in that mix.

"I hope I see some familiar faces tonight at the pub crawl."

The famous *pub crawl* in a town the size of Huckleberry Bay consists of roughly three bars, but it'll be fun to unwind after the race.

I hurry down the steps at the side of the stage to where my best friend, Zeke, is waiting.

"Why don't we come here more often?" he asks as we hurry toward the track. I slip my sunglasses onto my face and try to ignore the unfamiliar nervousness that's set up residence in my stomach.

I never get nervous.

Except, apparently, when I'm racing in my hometown.

"This town is fun. And beautiful. A little cold for being on the beach, but there are some good-looking women here, Wolfe."

"The race starts in thirty," I remind him. "Stop ogling the women and focus. You can ogle tonight."

"Oh, I plan to. There's a blonde who's caught my eye. Hopefully, she shows up later."

"Hopefully, she isn't married like that chick in Daytona."

I give my friend the side-eye, and he sighs, rubbing the back of his neck.

"Yeah, well, that wasn't entirely my fault. She didn't say she was married. Wasn't wearing a ring."

"Might be something you want to ask before you get them naked," I suggest as we approach the car. "Now, let's work on winning this race before we shift focus to other activities, shall we?"

"Of course, you're going to win," Zeke points out. "This is a dirt track. You're a stock car *champion*. These guys all do this as a hobby, and you've won more cups than I can count on two hands."

"Thanks for reciting my resume."

"You've got this in the bag. It's all to show off for your hometown and raise some money," he says with an arrogant grin. "But I'm not complaining. We needed some R&R."

"And we can start that after we finish *this*."

Twenty-six minutes later, after the national anthem's been sung and I've waved to the crowd some more, we're ready to go.

Ten laps in, the car is warming up nicely, and I'm pumped full of adrenaline and in the lead. Someone pulls up beside me on the straightaway and tries to cut me off, drifting around the corner. But they're too close. Way too damn close.

"Back off," I mutter, eyeing the other car in my mirror as I grip the wheel harder. "You're going to kill us, asshole."

The next thing I know, they've clipped my bumper with theirs, and I'm spinning, then rolling—at almost a hundred miles an hour. I see the wall coming for me.

And then I don't see anything at all.

About Kristen Proby

New York Times and USA Today bestselling author Kristen Proby has published more than seventy romance novels. She is best known for her self-published With Me In Seattle and Boudreaux series. Kristen lives in Montana with her husband, two cats, and a spoiled dog.

Discover 1001 Dark Nights

COLLECTION ONE
FOREVER WICKED by Shayla Black ~ CRIMSON TWILIGHT by
Heather Graham ~ CAPTURED IN SURRENDER by Liliana Hart ~
SILENT BITE: A SCANGUARDS WEDDING by Tina Folsom ~
DUNGEON GAMES by Lexi Blake ~ AZAGOTH by Larissa Ione ~
NEED YOU NOW by Lisa Renee Jones ~ SHOW ME, BABY by
Cherise Sinclair~ ROPED IN by Lorelei James ~ TEMPTED BY
MIDNIGHT by Lara Adrian ~ THE FLAME by Christopher Rice ~
CARESS OF DARKNESS by Julie Kenner

COLLECTION TWO
WICKED WOLF by Carrie Ann Ryan ~ WHEN IRISH EYES ARE
HAUNTING by Heather Graham ~ EASY WITH YOU by Kristen
Proby ~ MASTER OF FREEDOM by Cherise Sinclair ~ CARESS OF
PLEASURE by Julie Kenner ~ ADORED by Lexi Blake ~ HADES by
Larissa Ione ~ RAVAGED by Elisabeth Naughton ~ DREAM OF YOU
by Jennifer L. Armentrout ~ STRIPPED DOWN by Lorelei James ~
RAGE/KILLIAN by Alexandra Ivy/Laura Wright ~ DRAGON KING
by Donna Grant ~ PURE WICKED by Shayla Black ~ HARD AS
STEEL by Laura Kaye ~ STROKE OF MIDNIGHT by Lara Adrian ~
ALL HALLOWS EVE by Heather Graham ~ KISS THE FLAME by
Christopher Rice~ DARING HER LOVE by Melissa Foster ~ TEASED
by Rebecca Zanetti ~ THE PROMISE OF SURRENDER by Liliana
Hart

COLLECTION THREE
HIDDEN INK by Carrie Ann Ryan ~ BLOOD ON THE BAYOU by
Heather Graham ~ SEARCHING FOR MINE by Jennifer Probst ~
DANCE OF DESIRE by Christopher Rice ~ ROUGH RHYTHM by
Tessa Bailey ~ DEVOTED by Lexi Blake ~ Z by Larissa Ione ~
FALLING UNDER YOU by Laurelin Paige ~ EASY FOR KEEPS by
Kristen Proby ~ UNCHAINED by Elisabeth Naughton ~ HARD TO
SERVE by Laura Kaye ~ DRAGON FEVER by Donna Grant ~
KAYDEN/SIMON by Alexandra Ivy/Laura Wright ~ STRUNG UP by
Lorelei James ~ MIDNIGHT UNTAMED by Lara Adrian ~ TRICKED
by Rebecca Zanetti ~ DIRTY WICKED by Shayla Black ~ THE ONLY

ONE by Lauren Blakely ~ SWEET SURRENDER by Liliana Hart

COLLECTION FOUR
ROCK CHICK REAWAKENING by Kristen Ashley ~ ADORING
INK by Carrie Ann Ryan ~ SWEET RIVALRY by K. Bromberg ~
SHADE'S LADY by Joanna Wylde ~ RAZR by Larissa Ione ~
ARRANGED by Lexi Blake ~ TANGLED by Rebecca Zanetti ~
HOLD ME by J. Kenner ~ SOMEHOW, SOME WAY by Jennifer
Probst ~ TOO CLOSE TO CALL by Tessa Bailey ~ HUNTED by
Elisabeth Naughton ~ EYES ON YOU by Laura Kaye ~ BLADE by
Alexandra Ivy/Laura Wright ~ DRAGON BURN by Donna Grant ~
TRIPPED OUT by Lorelei James ~ STUD FINDER by Lauren Blakely
~ MIDNIGHT UNLEASHED by Lara Adrian ~ HALLOW BE THE
HAUNT by Heather Graham ~ DIRTY FILTHY FIX by Laurelin Paige
~ THE BED MATE by Kendall Ryan ~ NIGHT GAMES by CD Reiss
~ NO RESERVATIONS by Kristen Proby ~ DAWN OF
SURRENDER by Liliana Hart

COLLECTION FIVE
BLAZE ERUPTING by Rebecca Zanetti ~ ROUGH RIDE by Kristen
Ashley ~ HAWKYN by Larissa Ione ~ RIDE DIRTY by Laura Kaye ~
ROME'S CHANCE by Joanna Wylde ~ THE MARRIAGE
ARRANGEMENT by Jennifer Probst ~ SURRENDER by Elisabeth
Naughton ~ INKED NIGHTS by Carrie Ann Ryan ~ ENVY by Rachel
Van Dyken ~ PROTECTED by Lexi Blake ~ THE PRINCE by Jennifer
L. Armentrout ~ PLEASE ME by J. Kenner ~ WOUND TIGHT by
Lorelei James ~ STRONG by Kylie Scott ~ DRAGON NIGHT by
Donna Grant ~ TEMPTING BROOKE by Kristen Proby ~
HAUNTED BE THE HOLIDAYS by Heather Graham ~ CONTROL
by K. Bromberg ~ HUNKY HEARTBREAKER by Kendall Ryan ~
THE DARKEST CAPTIVE by Gena Showalter

COLLECTION SIX
DRAGON CLAIMED by Donna Grant ~ ASHES TO INK by Carrie
Ann Ryan ~ ENSNARED by Elisabeth Naughton ~ EVERMORE by
Corinne Michaels ~ VENGEANCE by Rebecca Zanetti ~ ELI'S
TRIUMPH by Joanna Wylde ~ CIPHER by Larissa Ione ~ RESCUING
MACIE by Susan Stoker ~ ENCHANTED by Lexi Blake ~ TAKE THE

BRIDE by Carly Phillips ~ INDULGE ME by J. Kenner ~ THE KING by Jennifer L. Armentrout ~ QUIET MAN by Kristen Ashley ~ ABANDON by Rachel Van Dyken ~ THE OPEN DOOR by Laurelin Paige ~ CLOSER by Kylie Scott ~ SOMETHING JUST LIKE THIS by Jennifer Probst ~ BLOOD NIGHT by Heather Graham ~ TWIST OF FATE by Jill Shalvis ~ MORE THAN PLEASURE YOU by Shayla Black ~ WONDER WITH ME by Kristen Proby ~ THE DARKEST ASSASSIN by Gena Showalter

COLLECTION SEVEN
THE BISHOP by Skye Warren ~ TAKEN WITH YOU by Carrie Ann Ryan ~ DRAGON LOST by Donna Grant ~ SEXY LOVE by Carly Phillips ~ PROVOKE by Rachel Van Dyken ~ RAFE by Sawyer Bennett ~ THE NAUGHTY PRINCESS by Claire Contreras ~ THE GRAVEYARD SHIFT by Darynda Jones ~ CHARMED by Lexi Blake ~ SACRIFICE OF DARKNESS by Alexandra Ivy ~ THE QUEEN by Jen Armentrout ~ BEGIN AGAIN by Jennifer Probst ~ VIXEN by Rebecca Zanetti ~ SLASH by Laurelin Paige ~ THE DEAD HEAT OF SUMMER by Heather Graham ~ WILD FIRE by Kristen Ashley ~ MORE THAN PROTECT YOU by Shayla Black ~ LOVE SONG by Kylie Scott ~ CHERISH ME by J. Kenner ~ SHINE WITH ME by Kristen Proby

COLLECTION EIGHT
DRAGON REVEALED by Donna Grant ~ CAPTURED IN INK by Carrie Ann Ryan ~ SECURING JANE by Susan Stoker ~ WILD WIND by Kristen Ashley ~ DARE TO TEASE by Carly Phillips ~ VAMPIRE by Rebecca Zanetti ~ MAFIA KING by Rachel Van Dyken ~ THE GRAVEDIGGER'S SON by Darynda Jones ~ FINALE by Skye Warren ~ MEMORIES OF YOU by J. Kenner ~ SLAYED BY DARKNESS by Alexandra Ivy ~ TREASURED by Lexi Blake ~ THE DAREDEVIL by Dylan Allen ~ BOND OF DESTINY by Larissa Ione ~ MORE THAN POSSESS YOU by Shayla Black ~ HAUNTED HOUSE by Heather Graham ~ MAN FOR ME by Laurelin Paige ~ THE RHYTHM METHOD by Kylie Scott ~ JONAH BENNETT by Tijan ~ CHANGE WITH ME by Kristen Proby ~ THE DARKEST DESTINY by Gena Showalter

COLLECTION NINE

DRAGON UNBOUND by Donna Grant ~ NOTHING BUT INK by Carrie Ann Ryan ~ THE MASTERMIND by Dylan Allen ~ JUST ONE WISH by Carly Phillips ~ BEHIND CLOSED DOORS by Skye Warren ~ GOSSAMER IN THE DARKNESS by Kristen Ashley ~ THE CLOSE-UP by Kennedy Ryan ~ DELIGHTED by Lexi Blake ~ THE GRAVESIDE BAR AND GRILL by Darynda Jones ~ THE ANTI-FAN AND THE IDOL by Rachel Van Dyken ~ CHARMED BY YOU by J. Kenner ~ DESCEND TO DARKNESS by Heather Graham~ BOND OF PASSION by Larissa Ione ~ JUST WHAT I NEEDED by Kylie Scott

Discover Blue Box Press

TAME ME by J. Kenner ~ TEMPT ME by J. Kenner ~ DAMIEN by J. Kenner ~ TEASE ME by J. Kenner ~ REAPER by Larissa Ione ~ THE SURRENDER GATE by Christopher Rice ~ SERVICING THE TARGET by Cherise Sinclair ~ THE LAKE OF LEARNING by Steve Berry and M.J. Rose ~ THE MUSEUM OF MYSTERIES by Steve Berry and M.J. Rose ~ TEASE ME by J. Kenner ~ FROM BLOOD AND ASH by Jennifer L. Armentrout ~ QUEEN MOVE by Kennedy Ryan ~ THE HOUSE OF LONG AGO by Steve Berry and M.J. Rose ~ THE BUTTERFLY ROOM by Lucinda Riley ~ A KINGDOM OF FLESH AND FIRE by Jennifer L. Armentrout ~ THE LAST TIARA by M.J. Rose ~ THE CROWN OF GILDED BONES by Jennifer L. Armentrout ~ THE MISSING SISTER by Lucinda Riley ~ THE END OF FOREVER by Steve Berry and M.J. Rose ~ THE STEAL by C. W. Gortner and M.J. Rose ~ CHASING SERENITY by Kristen Ashley ~ A SHADOW IN THE EMBER by Jennifer L. Armentrout ~ THE BAIT by C.W. Gortner and M.J. Rose ~ THE FASHION ORPHANS by Randy Susan Meyers and M.J. Rose ~ TAKING THE LEAP by Kristen Ashley ~ SAPPHIRE SUNSET by Christopher Rice writing C. Travis Rice ~ THE WAR OF TWO QUEENS by Jennifer L. Armentrout ~ THE MURDERS AT FLEAT HOUSE by Lucinda Riley ~ THE HEIST by C.W. Gortner and M.J. Rose ~ SAPPHIRE SPRING by Christopher Rice writing as C. Travis Rice ~ MAKING THE MATCH by Kristen Ashley ~ A LIGHT IN THE FLAME by Jennifer L.

On Behalf of 1001 Dark Nights,

Liz Berry, M.J. Rose, and Jillian Stein would like to thank ~

Steve Berry
Doug Scofield
Benjamin Stein
Kim Guidroz
Chelle Olson
Tanaka Kangara
Asha Hossain
Chris Graham
Jessica Saunders
Stacey Tardif
Dylan Stockton
Kate Boggs
Richard Blake
and Simon Lipskar

Printed in Great Britain
by Amazon

37846660R00061